MARVELS, MOCHAS, AND MURDER

COMICS AND COFFEE CASE FILES BOOK 1

CHRISTINE ZANE THOMAS
WILLIAM TYLER DAVIS

Edited by
ELLEN CAMPBELL

very day there was one, and today's had come early —with the very first customer. Of course, I use the word customer lightly—he hadn't bought anything, not yet. He just eyed the menu with a sort of skepticism.

I was getting used to these types: folks who looked at the shop like it belonged on another planet. See, I knew the problem. And I was ready to throw my hands up, to give up, and cut my co-owner Ryan from the business completely.

Ryan, I thought, gritting my teeth. This was *supposed* to be a partnership. Fifty-fifty. But he was nowhere to be seen. Not this early in the morning.

The guy continued his perusal while I just stood and watched his eyes flicker back and forth.

The menu wasn't different from any other coffee shop, not much different from a Starbucks, really.

The shop itself, well, that's a different story...

"A comic book *and* coffee shop," the guy finally said, grinning. "Or is it a coffee and comic shop?" The look he gave me indicated how perplexing the question truly was. Hint, hint: it wasn't perplexing in the least.

I shrugged and gave him my best tightlipped smile.

"It's cute, *really*. Kapow Koffee," he emphasized the misspelling of the word coffee. "I just had to see it."

Well now you've seen it, I thought. But I said, "Yeah, it's a real *novel* concept."

He chuckled at my lame joke.

In the months since the shop opened, this shtick was almost a weekly occurrence. And per usual, it was some rich guy from across the bay, either on vacation or just passing by the shop for the first time.

What a jerk, I thought snidely, my lips still pressed together with this smile.

"So, what're the specials?" he asked. He was an older man, maybe fifty-five. He wore a *Titleist* ball cap. His purple polo shirt was tucked into khaki shorts. White ankle socks inched over his golf shoes—the old school kind, white with a brown saddle in the center. The guy's chest hair poked out from beneath the unbuttoned collar of his shirt. His skin was red and splotchy from too much sun.

A golfer this time of morning wasn't necessarily unusual. We had a few regulars that liked to stop in on their way to the links. But this guy I didn't recognize. Not that it meant he wasn't a local. He very well could be. I'd grown up in Niilhaasi, but I'd spent the past almost ten years away. I'd only moved back last year.

Southeast of Tallahassee, the city itself was named after the bay—not vice versa. Niilhaasi Bay, a brackish mass of water, sat between us and the island. It was named by the Seminole tribe for the way the moon reflected on the water at night, Moon Bay.

Technically, Gaiman Island was also part of the city. Full

of condos, timeshares, weekend and summer homes of the rich, it may as well have been another part of the universe. The toll bridge was a dividing line between their mecca and the rest of us.

Sure, a sliver of public beach was available to all. We used it, if grudgingly. But the rest of the island was gated. The houses there sold for prices well into the millions. With its own private airstrip and services to pick up food and supplies from here across the bay, most of the island's inhabitants never need venture to *our* side of reality.

This guy was either a tourist or one of the part-time residents. Yes, Niilhaasi did get tourists from time to time but not in droves like the white sand beaches to the west in Panama City and Destin. Here, the sand was a cream color, and the water was only emerald about one day a month.

The sad fact—I was holding on to some hope that business would pick up now that summer had fully kicked in. Hope that guys like this one would head past the downtown strip on their way to one of Niilhaasi's many country clubs.

Now I was regretting that hope.

"Well," I told him, " there's a buy two bags get one free ground coffee special." I motioned to the assortment of ground coffees in their brown bags. "Or there's the—"

"No," he cut me off, his smile growing broader, "I meant the comic and coffee special." He pointed to the chalkboard sign at the entrance of the shop.

"Oh, uh, that?" I grimaced. To be honest, the comic book side of the store wasn't my idea. I'd only agreed to it because I had to. Coffee was my side of the house. I hadn't read a comic book since the 8th grade.

I reached under the counter, scanned the shelf. Then I grabbed an old issue of *Batman Detective Comics*.

"So," I ventured, "if you buy any specialty latte and an old comic from this shelf you get them *both* fifty percent off."

He eyed the shelf, then the menu. He crunched the numbers inside his head. "That's the same price as a latte," he confirmed.

My hold on the comic's outer plastic bag was already slipping as I readied to put it back.

"I think I'll just take the latte." He laughed like we were both in on some inside joke.

"Sure. I understand." I put the comic back under the counter and went to make his coffee.

"And Kirby," he found my name tag, "can you add a pump or two of vanilla?"

"Sure thing," I said. I gave him another fake smile.

The trick to a good latte was in making the shots—any idiot can froth milk—but getting each shot to perfection is a skill. The ground espresso should be compact enough for the water to seep through, but not too compact or it makes the espresso extra bitter. I knew the shot was a good one when the machine poured the tricolor layers of black, golden brown, and cream.

Like I said before, coffee is my thing. And it's what I moved back to Niilhaasi to do.

I set the vanilla latte down on the counter, nodding toward the customer—and he was a customer. He did pay, after all.

He grabbed it up and took the first sip hesitantly like he was expecting it to taste of comic book. It didn't.

He nodded, turning away. Then the guy stopped in his tracks, took another sip, and turned back to me. "That's a helluva good coffee."

I gave him a knowing smile, watching as the corners of his cheeks slid into a grin. Shaking his head, the customer took one last sip before leaving the shop. His face hovered inches over the lid of the cup, never truly putting the coffee down between mouthfuls.

The bell, dangling beneath the door handle, jingled twice.

That same bell jingled softly a few hours later. Ryan, his arms full with two brown paper sacks from the Chinese takeout down the street, entered the shop. He flashed an all-too-familiar broad smile my way.

Per usual, he was late.

A leash hung from his wrist. Attached to it was Ryan's dapple dachshund. The dog padded ahead, then shook his floppy ears. The sound of his tags shaking echoed in the quiet shop—which reminded me that I'd forgotten to put on the sound system.

"I know you're ready to be free," Ryan acknowledged the dog. He set the takeout on one of the many *empty* booths and bent over to unclasp Gambit's leash. To Ryan's credit, the dog did appreciate the gesture. He bounded away to his dog bed which sat beneath a comic display case at the edge of the shop. Then he burrowed under the ratty blanket on top of it.

Kapow Koffee was located on Main Street. The city had essentially allowed us, and a few other establishments, to move in for free and renovate the building. This was in hopes we'd invest *our* money into the rundown space and renew vigor in the community. Just like they'd seen so many other small towns do with success.

The first part happened almost exactly as they had planned. We sank our funds into reinventing what in the

1960s had been an appliance store. The second part of the city's plan, well, it was still a work in progress. Downtown was dead in the morning, dead at night, and the lunch hour was less a rush and more a trickle.

But the money invested did give the shop a decent coffee shop vibe—exposed brick, antique wooden tables, dim lighting. Eight booths made up the center of the shop: four and four, divided by a small wooden wall. Anyone could curl inside a booth with a laptop and coffee. They could sit for hours on the Wi-Fi and either work or play.

And our few regulars did just that.

Alan's face was aglow about three inches from his laptop. His massive headphones looked like earmuffs you'd find in the Arctic north, Bluetooth, no cables to indicate their purpose.

Another regular, Karen, at least glanced up at Gambit's entrance. But she went quickly back to whatever she did on the phone while she perused Facebook on the tablet beside the MacBook that she barely used. Her booth slash worksta-tion was always filled with gadgets and cords. I'd literally bought a power strip just for her booth. She put her finger to the MacBook's trackpad every few minutes to keep the screen awake. She sipped her coffee a bit more often.

This was *our* shop. Half coffee—me. Half comics—Ryan. And as much as I wanted to, there was no hiding the comic book display shelves just past the booths or the figurines locked in a display case above the bar.

Ryan took a seat in the booth closest to the door where he'd set down the food. Hesitantly, I did the same, sliding in opposite him.

"You know we open at 6:00," I said for my own benefit.

"No," he argued, "the comic store opens at 11:00."

"It's 11:22."

"I had to get us food."

"Us?" I never knew if he was referring to me or the dog. Gambit sensed this and perked up, ears a twitch.

"Yeah, us. I got you General Tso's." Ryan grinned. The pathway to my forgiveness would always be through my stomach.

Ryan had been my best friend since the sixth grade when my parents decided to move across town. Instead of going to middle school with my elementary school friends, I was forced to make new ones.

Lucky for me, Ryan was in a similar situation. He'd just moved to Niilhaasi Bay from Michigan. His father had retired from GM.

He was an "oopsie baby." The youngest of three. Ryan's brother and sister were in college at the time of the move. His parents were a generation older than everyone else's. They'd saved their whole lives to retire to Florida, and they weren't going to let a twelve-year-old stop that train.

After high school, we went our separate ways. I joined the Air Force to see the world, and I did get to see a bit of it. Ryan flunked out of two colleges before he made his way back home to his parents' now vacant house.

"You sell any comics this morning?" he asked me between bites of sweet and sour chicken.

"I, uh, I tried." I shrugged.

"Do or do not." Ryan said in his best Yoda impression.

"I don't know, man. This comics thing. It's just—" I sighed. "When you talked me into this whole endeavor, I thought maybe I'd have some help."

"Hey! I do help! Just not in the a.m. And in fairness, I told you from the beginning I wasn't a morning person."

"I know," I said, flustered. I put down the white box of takeout. The next part came out reluctantly. "It's just your side of the business—it isn't really pulling its weight. In fact, it's kind of a distraction—a deterrent almost."

This had been coming for months. But every time I brought it up, Ryan pushed harder, digging his heels in. He was unwilling to hear it.

"No one knows what they're getting into when they walk through that door," I continued. "Kapow Koffee—it sounded cool a few months ago. But the finances aren't adding up."

"Harsh, bro." Ryan put down his white carton but still gripped the chopsticks tightly in his right hand. "Kirby," he said defensively, "you're the one who couldn't get the business loan without additional collateral."

"Right," I hesitated. "And you're the one who had to have a comic shop for doing nothing but put your parents' house up against it. I'm not sure that was a fair trade—especially if it sinks the business and costs you that house. I'm trying to look out for you in this as well."

"Sure you are." Ryan narrowed his eyes. They were a pale blue, a stark contrast to my brown, nearly black irises. He went back to his food and said, "For today, man, can you cut me some slack? I'm grieving."

"Grieving? Grieving over what?"

"Robin dumped me the other night."

"Robin?" I questioned.

"You know." He sighed like we'd had this conversation before. It was true, we'd had conversations just like it.

Ryan eyed the rest of the shop for anyone listening. If Alan's music was off, we'd never know it. But the guy stared intently at his screen like the fate of the world depended on him debugging the software problem of the day. Ryan lowered his voice anyway. "Come on," he said. "You know, the one with the husband."

"Oh, her?" I asked nonchalantly, my voice at the regular

level. In reality, the reminder hit me like a gut punch. I was no stranger to cheating. Cheating was fifty percent of the reason I was back in Niilhaasi in the first place.

"Yeah, her," he said. "But as far as I know she hasn't said anything to her husband about us. So at least there's that. And the kicker is, he was cheating, too. I guess they're gonna try and work it out. Two cheaters, yeah, I'm sure it'll all end well. Still, Robin is hot. It'd be nice if we could meet every now and again and, uh—"

"Don't say it," I cut him off.

"But she *is* super hot."

I rolled my eyes.

Ryan shrugged and went back to eating.

It was strange, but Ryan was basically the local playboy. Not because he was so handsome—average height, average weight. His reddish brown hair was two shades lighter than my own.

What made him desirable, I guess, was that he never changed. The guy looked the same as the day we graduated. Add to that he was thirty and single with no kids, no attachments of any kind.

All the jocks we graduated with either got married or gained weight or both—usually both.

I had similar things going for me. Not too much weight gain, either. But the crows were scratching at the corners of my eyes. And I had to go to the gym and eat half as much as I wanted while Ryan, here, devoured a whole order of sweet and sour chicken with two cartons of fried rice.

But I wasn't ready to go back in the dating pool. Not yet.

"So, what do you have planned for the rest of the day?" Ryan cleaned up the mess while I brewed more coffee. We usually had a rush in the early afternoon—the local kids all coming home from a morning at the beach.

I opened my palms out to the shop. "You're looking at it."

"No, I mean after work."

"I'm supposed to eat dinner with Memaw. But that's about it."

"You should come back to the shop tonight." He grinned manically. "Play some D&D with us. It'll be just like old times."

"Old times," I said. *Really old times*, I thought.

"Dude, you never want to play anymore! And it's not like you have a life. Watching reruns up there in your man-cave is not a life."

"Thanks."

"You know I didn't mean it like that."

"Well," I said, "some of us prefer to date single women and not play dungeon master when it's that or go to sleep alone."

"Oh, don't worry about me. I don't ever sleep 'alone.'"

I looked at the dog and grinned.

"Well, him, too." Ryan smiled. "But I've got a hot date tonight after the game."

"After the game?"

"Don't judge! She works late."

"Sure she does."

I pressed the button on the coffee grinder, drowning out Ryan's retort.

2

R ight on time, the high school crowd piled in and ordered their caffeine concoctions—blended drinks that tasted more like a melted candy bar than coffee. They added sweetener to the already delicious cold brew and picked over the comics with no intention of buying.

Their broke friends who tagged along for rides and handouts drank our water for free. They were all just loud enough to drive the morning regulars back to their homes. Even Allan with his ginormous headphones wasn't immune.

At around 2:00 one of Kapow Koffee's few employees, Sarah, came in and relieved me of my barista duties. This allowed me to do the "fun" managerial work required of the cafe. Making the schedule, ordering pastries, paying bills, all these things so easily fell to the wayside if I didn't stay on top of it myself.

Customers, of course, always took precedence. But the first month we were open, I let a lot of little things take priority over bigger ones. Things like deficient mopping—

streaks on the tile (it's a thing)—got me sidetracked from the hour designated for payroll.

I suffered the consequences that month, mostly in lack of sleep. I'd startle awake in the middle of the night remembering some task I'd forgotten.

Luckily, my studio apartment was above the shop. And doubly lucky, there was always coffee around to get me through the remainder of the day.

I sidestepped past Ryan between the cash register and the espresso machine on my way toward the office.

Sarah was a tall, blonde girl two years out of high school. A theater major at the University of Central Florida, she was home for the summer. I could smell the sunscreen from her morning at the beach. She greeted me with a shy smile, donning a black apron. I couldn't help noticing her name tag now had more than just her name. Below it in permanent ink it read, "Ask me about Captain Marvel."

I rolled my eyes. "Did Ryan put you up to that? You know he's barely your boss. You don't have to wear that."

She looked down, confused. "Oh, this? No. He sent me home with a few graphic novels the other night. And he's right. She's a badass."

"She is? I thought *she* was a he—Shazam or something."

"That's the DC version, though I think Marvel had a couple of dudes before Carole Danvers. But Carole's the badass."

"I'm sure she is." I chuckled.

The next couple of hours were a blur. I went through my chores without paying much attention to the storefront, though I tended to smile when the bell on the door jingled. The sound of customers was always a welcome one.

Every so often I heard Ryan drone on with one of *his* customers, picking up their file of comics the shop held by request. This was one of my points of contention with Ryan. We stored these books out of sight, and some customers let their file grow to several hundred dollars' worth of merchandise before picking them up. Even then, they might not buy the whole stack—putting *us* in the hole.

But it was Ryan's element. I let him manage it.

His long-winded chats about the new Marvel or DC movies, Star Wars, or anything else Sci-Fi and Fantasy were a fixture this time of the afternoon. The shop wouldn't sound the same without them.

So, I wasn't surprised to hear his voice. I was, however, surprised at the tone echoing through the store. Gambit wasn't used to it either. The dog joined in, growling low— telling me something was definitely off.

The dachshund hardly ever barked—except at thunder. His guttural growl sounded like that of a bigger dog, and it had never found its way to my office before.

I paused, resting my fingers on my laptop's keyboard, listening.

"It's not for sale," I heard Ryan say loudly. It was like he was trying to call me out there.

The response to his words I couldn't make out.

I stood and poked my head out of the office doorway, but Ryan and Sarah were all I could see.

"I said it's not for sale," Ryan repeated himself.

Sighing, I walked back into the store front. "What's not for sale?"

As far I was concerned everything in the shop was for sale. Well, almost everything. My only quibble would be if someone was trying to buy Gambit.

"Kirby," the customer sighed with relief, "tell him to stop being a jerk and just sell it." I recognized the customer instantly. Then I understood *why* Ryan was acting the way he was.

Corey Ottley was our age. He was a bit more muscular than I remembered him from high school. He had sandy blonde hair which he gelled into a wave above his wide forehead. A thin nose, a square jaw, earrings in both ears.

Corey gave me a relieved smile, then he pointed up to the top shelf behind me—the place Ryan kept the more valuable action figures and toys. I turned back to look at it.

There, on the shelf, was a large figure, statue or bust—whatever it's called, of Captain America. And not the one from the movies, although we had one of those, too. No, this one was based on the comic books.

"It's not for sale." Ryan shrugged.

It *was* for sale. I could see the price sticker on the bottom, magnified by the glass shelf it sat atop. *Two hundred dollars*—I nearly choked.

"I'm offering more than asking price," Corey said to me. "Kirby, please tell Ryan to see reason."

He turned back to Ryan. "And dude, it was ten years ago. Move on."

"Over ten years ago," I corrected.

Sarah was smart enough to inch back out of the way as Ryan spun toward Corey with fire in his eyes. "No, dude," he said. "You beat me up. I'm not forgiving you."

"Beat you up?" Corey protested. "I threw one punch! And if I recall correctly, it was justified. You said I was a Trekkie nerd who'd never move out of his mother's basement. And speaking of, don't you live in your mother's basement?"

"We live in Florida," Ryan argued. "There are no basements. Besides, I live in the whole house."

"And actually," I interrupted, cringing as I told the truth

for the first time in over ten years, "it was me who said those things."

It felt good to finally come clean. Ryan had taken the punch, one I'd truly deserved.

"Really?" Corey's face fell.

I instinctively backed away.

"Kirby," Corey put a hand up in protest, "I'm not going to sucker punch you. Like you said, that was over ten years ago. But you could, however, sell me that figure."

Ryan stepped between us. "It's still not for sale."

"All right. Final offer. Two fifty."

"All right. Final refusal," Ryan said. "No."

"Kirby?" Corey pleaded.

Of course, I knew this was about more than one punch. Corey was in our circle of friends throughout high school— well, up until that day. The fight had honestly been brewing for years. Both Ryan and Corey had pined after the same girl, Jill Thompson. And one lucky day, Corey scored a date with her.

My offhand comment was a lousy attempt to console Ryan—one overheard by our mutual friend Marc. Then high school did what it did best. It created drama over what amounted to nothing. Corey's date with Jill was singular, and Ryan had found his first long-term girlfriend less than a week later, a girl named Gertrude if I recalled correctly.

I put my hands up. "Sorry, man," I told Corey, "but this is Ryan's side of the store. I'm happy to sell you a coffee or something. In fact, you can have a cup on the house."

"Ow!" Ryan elbowed my ribs.

"You know what. Eff it," Corey barked. He shook his head and stormed out of the shop. Before the door closed behind him, he yelled something like, "You'll be seeing my review online."

It was my turn to fix Ryan with a cold stare.

"Really?"

"Really," he replied snidely. "Corey knows he can get one on eBay for half this price. He just wanted to come in and taunt me."

"Taunt you?" I scoffed. "It seemed like he wanted to come in and give you money in exchange for that POS figure."

"Hey! Don't talk about Cap that way... But no. He wanted to come in and show *us* just how much money he's worth these days. You saw the hair, the clothes," Ryan pointed outside, "the Corvette."

A yellow Corvette slid back out of the angled parking in front of the store. It jetted off, its engine humming aggressively.

I bit my lip.

I hadn't really noticed any of it. But now that I did, I wondered exactly where all Corey's money had come from.

3

My grandmother—that is, Memaw—lived only a few miles north of the downtown strip. With no view of the shore, she barely got an ocean breeze in the summer. Tall pines surrounded her secluded double lot. The house was a white coastal cottage—again, not really by the coast but miles from the bay. My grandfather had built it with his own hands.

Memaw loved the house, though the house didn't seem to love Memaw. Since my Pawpaw's death, it was constantly giving her fits. If the air conditioning wasn't out, it was a plumbing leak, or a faulty light switch. In the last two months I had fixed or mended or replaced something every week.

So, I wasn't all that surprised to find something amiss when I got there that evening.

"Memaw?" I drawled. It was a Southern thing. Niilhaasi might claim Florida on the map, but I'd always thought of this place as lower Georgia. And the door was open—it always was. This wasn't the type of town where anyone needed to lock their doors at night.

"I'm in the kitchen, sweetie," Memaw called out.

I found her on the floor beside the sink, peering under it with a head lamp strapped on her head.

"Oh, no. What's up?" I asked.

"The garbage disposal," she said, matter-of-factly. "It's on the fritz."

"Define fritz... Did you drop a fork down there?"

"Kirby Jackson! Do I look that dumb to you?"

"Well," I grinned, "define dumb. What are you doing down there with the flashlight? Are you going to beam it back into good repair?"

"I was—I was going to... Just help me up," she huffed.

I did.

After I unclogged the garbage disposal with the end of a wooden spoon, I poured some baking soda, then some vinegar, and finally some boiling water down the sink to clean it out.

"I don't know what I'd do without you," she said after, hugging me tight around the shoulder.

"You'd probably just have Handy Hank on speed dial." I surveyed the kitchen. There were no signs of pots or pans on the stove. "So, uh, what's for dinner?"

"Oh, Kirb, I'm sorry. I lost track of time. What would you say to The Fish Camp? My treat."

"Your treat?" I waved my hand with a flourish. "After you, Madame."

My grandfather's death had played a big part in my move back. Two years before his passing, my parents had decided to up and move to Costa Rica, which according to my dad, was my mother's dream. I'd never heard her mention it before.

When Pawpaw died, it left Memaw all alone. But that wasn't the only thing he'd left. He'd also left a significant sum of money in my bank account for me.

So, rather than squander that money, I decided to open my dream business: a coffee shop.

The Fish Camp was a local eatery down on the harbor. An institution, it not only had the best seafood in town but was probably in contention for best in the state. We pulled into the parking lot. It wasn't made of gravel. Instead, it was mostly sand and thousands of oyster shells.

In addition to the local catches of the day, there was plenty of creole fare like crawfish pie and gumbo. When Pawpaw was alive, we'd come down every Wednesday night for the special: half off the Slurpin' Oyster Platter—twenty-four oysters, served in up to four styles with choice of raw, garlic and lemon butter, or my favorite, the cheddar jalapeño. Pawpaw had liked them champagne broiled.

Per usual, it was a packed house, but we found a seat outside on the patio where the smell of saltwater stung my nostrils. Memaw decided on the fried grouper sandwich. I couldn't say no to cobia, a fish so fine all it needed was a little salt, pepper, and butter to drive my taste buds wild. It wasn't often on the menu this late in the year—cobia season being only a few months in the spring.

Several other locals were out enjoying the night, some on dates. I recognized Karen Beecher from my high school graduating class. She had two little ones running amok, ducking under her table, and climbing the wood railing before her husband swooped over to keep them from falling.

Behind them, a woman who was seated at a table with a

man kept giving me a cold stare. Her eyes bored into me so hard I could feel them. Each time I glanced over, she looked away as if it was nothing.

It took a while for me to finally get a good look. Then I realized who she was—Robin, Ryan's *new* ex-girlfriend. And I decided the man across from her must be her husband. I didn't recognize him. But he, too, turned and side-eyed me from time to time. *Had she come clean about the affair?*

Leaving, they had to pass our table. The whole way across the wooden deck her eyes were fixed on me, her lips in a sneer. *What did I do wrong?* Well, besides maintain a friendship with the town playboy. But even that was on the rocks.

"Kirby?" Memaw waved her hand in front of my face. "You all right?"

"Yeah, sorry. I was just thinking of something."

She smiled, something she hadn't done as often since my Pawpaw passed. I let her twist my arm into sharing a slice of peanut butter pie. And by the time we left, I was so stuffed I was sure not to wake up on my first alarm the next morning.

"Five a.m. comes early," I told her as I dropped her off back at her house.

"Do you really have customers come in at six?" she asked.

"No," I said honestly. "But one day we will."

4

Ryan and his crew of minions were the last people I wanted to see before bed. I snuck in through the back entrance but peeked around into the storefront at the sound of their laughter, grunting, and farting. The tabletop dungeon was in full swing. They huddled together in one of the booths.

I smiled, despite myself. Even if we did shutter the comic side of the shop, I thought I'd still let him have his game nights.

The crew was made up of Ryan, our high school buddy Marc Drake, this kid Damian who might still be in high school—I wasn't sure—and Tim Grayson, a middle aged man with graying hair and a mustache. He wore the same faded blue t-shirt I'd seen him wear every time he came in the shop.

"I'm going to need a strength check," Ryan announced.

I watched as Tim rolled the twenty-sided die, and then he did a fist-pump—it must've been a good roll.

"Nice," Ryan said. "You're able to chop the tree down

with two swings of your ax and provide enough firewood to get the party through the night. And you guys are sure you want to build a fire, right?"

Ryan looked up and found me.

"Kirb, what's up? You ready to join us?"

Gambit, alerted to my presence, bolted over. He wasn't looking as sluggish as he did in the afternoon. I guess with all the excitement of Dungeons and Dragons, he was ready to play, too. A faded yellow tennis ball jutted halfway out of his mouth. I tugged it free and bounced it down the length of the store. It only took three bounces before the dog yanked it from the air.

"Nice catch," I told him, thinking Ryan wasn't the only one to talk to the dog.

"So, what'd'ya say?" Ryan asked again.

"We've already started," Damian remarked. When I looked at the kid, he wouldn't make eye contact.

"That's all right," Ryan said, grinning, "he can come across your campfire in the middle of the night. I think I have another character sheet written up around here some-where... And a miniature." Ryan held up a miniature figu-rine of what looked like a wizard with a staff.

Gambit came back to me with the ball. I threw it again.

"Hold up. We haven't decided on the fire yet," Marc interrupted. But he nodded to me and gave a smirk. He was only saying it for Damian's benefit. The young kid was already flustered for some reason, pouty even.

"Come on, Damian," insisted Ryan. "Now you won't be the only one playing a new character tonight."

"Fine." Damian sighed, his face flushed. He crumpled the edge of his character sheet. "And I guess I'm fine with the fire if you guys are."

"A fire works for me," Tim agreed.

Ryan looked at me expectantly.

"No, that's all right. Maybe next time." I waved and gave Gambit a little pat before throwing the ball one last time. "Y'all have a good night."

Before Ryan could mount a protest, I went up the stairs to my apartment, turned on the TV, and fell asleep to my favorite show.

I woke to the brightly lit television screen. It wasn't unusual for me—my problem with the sleep timer is when I know it's on, I tend to stay up for it.

While the TV was on, something else was definitely off. I heard a dog bark. *Had it only been an hour or so since I fell asleep?* I checked my phone. It was 4 a.m. *What's Gambit still doing in the shop at 4 a.m.? I'm going to kill Ryan,* I thought.

The dog barked again, urgently, or so it sounded. And if I wasn't mistaken, I heard the faint jingle of the front door's bell.

Maybe Ryan left, I thought—I hoped. I wanted to get back to sleep.

But Gambit barked again.

Groaning, I wiped the sleep from my eyes. I was going to have to get up a whole hour before my alarm. This day wasn't off to a good start. *I'm definitely going to kill Ryan,* I thought again.

At least living above a coffee shop had benefits. Wake up and there was the earthy scent of coffee wafting heavenly about in the air. We roasted our own beans. Not a heavy dark roast like most people are used to these days, but a precisely timed and delicately controlled burn of medium roast coffee. The lighter the roast, the more acidic. The darker, the more bitter. I wanted our coffee that perfect in-between flavor.

I drank in the aroma while pulling on a shirt and shorts to go downstairs.

Out in the hallway, the aroma grew stronger. The very best thing about living above the shop—I was only a flight of stairs away from a $6,000 espresso machine. I don't care how good you can make a latte at home, you're never going to do $6,000 machine good. It's a whole other level. And believe it or not, ours was a base model—they only get better. It was one of the few things in the shop I bought brand new—a worthwhile investment, unlike the massive comic book display case.

I took the stairs by two, still wondering what the hell was going on. What greeted me only left more questions. The pocket door to the storefront was closed. Gambit barely gave me any notice. He pawed and scratched at the door.

"What's going on, boy?" Sighing, I realized I was talking to the dog yet again. But why would Ryan lock him in here? None of this was making any sense.

I slid the door open—Gambit had nearly done so himself, nudging at the pocket door with dogged determination and his long nose. The dog raced from behind the counter and into the center of the shop.

My heart began hammering for no reason whatsoever. Or so I thought.

I edged up to the counter. Unthinking, I reached behind me to pull down a coffee mug. That's when I saw the body.

Ryan lay flat on his stomach in the walkway between the front counter and the door to the shop. A knife was stabbed crookedly into his back. He wasn't moving. Gambit licked at his face.

My hold on the coffee mug grew limp, and it shattered on the floor around my feet.

5

The next few minutes were a blur. I called 911, and the operator had me stay on the line until the emergency personnel arrived. I didn't know Niil-haasi had so many cops, especially on duty this early in the morning. The first to arrive were two uniformed officers, followed by two more, and then finally an ambulance, and a fire truck.

In the commotion, I had grabbed ahold of Gambit—possibly because the operator told me to do so, possibly because I knew it couldn't be a good thing to allow the dog to continue tampering with the scene of a crime. I held him closely. Tears rolled down my cheek. It's safe to say I was in a state of shock.

One officer took the dog from me, another two escorted me to the back of their vehicle. They didn't say much, but it only took a moment for me to realize I was their suspect.

"Sir, did you participate in the murder?" one asked.

"No," I said, shaking my head.

The other pushed me hard in the back "helping me" into their waiting vehicle.

"All right," the first said dismissively. "We've got to get this scene locked down. A detective will be by shortly to ask you some questions. If you could wait here in the vehicle..." he trailed off.

I just shrugged. There was no use in resisting, pleading my innocence. Not only was I not the confrontational type, but of the emotions building inside me, fear wasn't one of them. Not yet. I wasn't done processing Ryan's death. I wasn't ready to put up my own fight. Only a minute or so later I realized that it could've been my last moments of freedom.

Time passed slowly in the backseat of that patrol car. What was probably half an hour stretched and felt more like two or three. I watched as more teams arrived. Officers cordoned off the area. Some jotted down notes in small notepads while others took photos of the scene.

I wish I could say in those moments I'd done something constructive. Like the hero from my favorite show, *Castle*, I could've tried analyzing the crime scene, racking my brain for suspects. But I felt numb.

A rapping on the window woke me from the half-dazed stupor. I wiped drool from my chin, staring up at the shadowy figure outside the door. The sun was just now peeking over the horizon. There was a glow of orange light poking through the dark pines to the east.

The door opened. A familiar voice cried out, "Kirby?"

"Felicia?"

"Detective Strong," an officer beside her said, "do you know this guy?"

"Yeah, I do."

Felicia Strong looked exactly as I remembered her. Well, not exactly. My mental image of her was in a blue cap and gown with a golden tassel and white honors ribbons. The woman who barricaded my exit from the vehicle was in a smart women's suit. Beneath the light jacket a starched maroon button up shirt had a collar so sharp it could cut bread. Her crinkly dark hair was pulled back but still poofed out behind her thin neck. Her chestnut brown eyes stared down at me in contemplation.

She was reading me. Everything I said or did from here on out would be judged as truth or lie.

"Is it going to be a problem?" the other detective asked. He, too, wore plainclothes, but looked nowhere near as sharp as Felicia. His clothes were loose-fitting like he'd recently lost weight.

"Kirby, this is Detective Ross." She turned to him briefly. "No, it's not going to be a problem. Kirby, you can step out over here to the side of the building. We have some questions we're going to ask you here. But there's a real possibility we're going to have to take you back to the station later."

Detective Ross gave her a hard look which she returned with a roll of her eyes.

Felicia Strong was in her element. I'd never seen her quite like this. But it wasn't all that surprising. Becoming a cop had been her dream. But I thought she'd probably grow out of it. Her parents had always encouraged her otherwise. Her older brother was a cop—or he had been.

Felicia led me over to underneath the awning of one of the neighboring boutiques.

I could count on one hand—on one finger—how many times I'd been inside Jenny's Scrapbooking. But Jenny, that is Jen, was a regular customer—caramel macchiato, no whip, sugar-free vanilla syrup.

Detective Ross pulled an outside table and a chair over from the restaurant two shops down. Then he went into an unmarked car and pulled out a laptop.

"So, let's start with this morning and work back," Felicia said, almost to herself. "Kirby, can you tell us what happened this morning?"

I nodded. Then I explained about hearing Gambit, going downstairs and finding him locked up outside the storefront. Next, I told them how I found the body, about the knife protruding from out of Ryan's back, the blood on the floor, how cold he was to the touch when I checked for a pulse.

Felicia questioned. Detective Ross typed. And I answered.

"This knife in *the deceased's* back, did it look familiar to you?"

I bit my lip and nodded. I couldn't help but think how wrong the words she used to describe Ryan felt—the deceased. Only yesterday, he was full of life.

Felicia knew Ryan, too, but mostly through me. While Ryan had pined after Jill Thompson, Felicia was my high school crush. And weirdly, even in this setting, those feelings came flooding up toward the surface.

"And?" she prodded.

"It's the bread knife we use to cut bagels."

"You think it is or you know it is?" Detective Ross cut in.

"I, uh, I know it is." Before they had time to ask, I explained, "I thought it looked familiar, so while I was on the phone with the 911 operator, I checked behind the counter. It was missing."

"Was anything else missing?" Felicia asked. "Do you think this was a robbery?"

"No, I, uh, I don't know. I didn't check."

"Do you think your fingerprints are gonna be on that knife?" Detective Ross asked. He readied to close his computer for some reason.

"Probably." I shrugged. "We all use it—even Ryan."

"Are you suggesting—"

"Sorry," I said, flustered, "I'm not suggesting anything."

"Listen, Kirby," Felicia put herself between me and Detective Ross defensively, "we're going to take you to the station now. Once everything here is processed, we can go through the store and see if anything was stolen. You understand that's not the priority right now."

"Yeah, I do."

"Is there anyone I should call? Your folks? A lawyer?"

"My Memaw."

"Your Memaw?" Detective Ross laughed.

Felicia rolled her eyes. "It's not funny, Alex. We'll have your Memaw meet us down there. You mind getting in the back?" She opened the back door of their unmarked vehicle, a forest green Chevy Impala. I got in.

As Felicia shut the door, I heard Detective Ross ask, "Why isn't it funny?"

I couldn't hear her response. But I imagined it went something like this: "Because Kirby's Memaw was the paralegal to Niilhaasi's most powerful lawyer for thirty years."

The room the detectives placed me in was vaguely reminiscent of the interrogation rooms seen on TV and movies. But only vaguely. It wasn't a cold steel blue or gray, instead the walls were a cream color. And there wasn't a two-way mirror.

There was, however, a set of bars on the table between me and the detectives—a place to cuff a suspect. Luckily, I wasn't in handcuffs. Not yet. Another obvious addition to the room was the camera mounted in the corner.

Again, Detective Ross brought in his laptop. He fell into a seat opposite me and circled his fingers on the trackpad to wake the computer.

Aside from the differences in the room, it went almost as I expected it would. Detective Ross read me my rights. Asked if I wanted a lawyer. Said I was being detained, not arrested. Like a zombie, I complied with everything they said. I was equal parts numb and panicked.

By the looks of the detectives, they both assumed Morrison Grantley, Niilhaasi's well known defense attorney, would come striding in the station any minute now to shut me up.

Felicia offered me water and coffee—which I agreed to eagerly. Thoughts of my latte, the nutty flavor of the Kapow Koffee espresso, were all it took to send my head spinning once more. I wondered what had happened to Ryan? None of it made sense.

I drank their bitter brew, hoping caffeine would help to find the answers.

"Are you sure you don't want to wait for a lawyer?" Felicia asked again.

I said, "I'm sure." But my insides weren't exactly aligned with that judgment.

"Okay," she said grimly. Then Felicia looked up to the camera as if to ensure it was on. "Your name is Kirby Jackson, correct?"

"Correct."

"And your relationship with *the deceased*, Ryan Walker, is what?"

"Friends since middle school." I shrugged. "And co-workers."

"You own Kapow Koffee on Main Street?"

"Yes. We both did."

"And what was *the deceased's* role there? What did he do as owner?"

"Uh, he did the comic book side. I do coffee."

She nodded. "I see." Felicia gave me another grim look. "Kirby, out of courtesy, I'm going to tell you that we're beginning the process of securing a search warrant for your apartment upstairs—and for the coffee shop's books, your laptop, all of that kind of stuff. You understand?"

I nodded. I'd seen enough *Castle* to know how this was going to play out.

"Can you tell us about the last time you saw Mr. Walker alive?"

I explained about the D&D game back at the shop.

"Can I get the names of the other players again?" Detective Ross asked. This time, he scribbled them in a notepad.

"Sure," I answered, "Marc Drake, this guy named Tim Grayson, and I don't know his last name, but a kid named Damian."

"Kid?" Ross questioned.

"Sorry. He's high school or college age."

"Right."

"I know Marc," Felicia announced. "We can run by his place after this."

Detective Ross gave her a curt nod as he went back to his laptop keyboard.

"All right," Felicia turned back to me, "so this is the important bit. If it really wasn't you, do you know anyone who wanted to harm Mr. Walker? Is there anything he said or did to indicate—"

"Well," I interrupted, "he did just go through a breakup of sorts." My mind went back to the cold stare of Robin Snider back at The Fish Camp. "And I think he was supposed to meet someone after D&D."

"Who?" both detectives asked quickly.

I shrugged. "He didn't say."

Detective Ross took out his phone and texted someone.

"Tell me more about the breakup," Felicia said.

I told them the little I knew about Robin—she was married, and she wanted to work it out with her husband. Something told me not to say anything about seeing her the previous night.

A few moments later, there was a knock at the door. A uniformed officer handed Detective Ross a plastic bag, in it was Ryan's cell phone. He set it down on the table between us.

"You don't happen to know the code for this thing, do you?"

"Ryan usually uses his thumbprint." I shrugged but wondered if that sounded bad—like I was suggesting they use a dead man's thumb. I rushed to say, "But maybe you could try one two three four."

Over the plastic, Detective Ross hit the home button and typed in the numbers.

Felicia almost laughed when it opened. "Really? They didn't try one two three four?"

Ross smirked. "I think they tried all ones and all nines before giving up."

"So, what was this guy's deal?" Detective Ross asked me. His thumb was swiping up and down through Ryan's contact list. "Hardly anyone in here is listed by name. There's four different iterations of 'Hot Bar Chick.' There's a Married Robin—I'm guessing that's the one we were just talking about—and a hawt Kristie with a K, hot spelled H A W T. There's even a MILF 1 and MILF 2."

Ross gave Felicia a weird look. *Does she have a kid?* If so, I thought she would definitely qualify.

"It's not me," she said defensively.

Ross smiled. "So, what was his deal?" he asked again.

"His deal? He just dated a lot."

"I see." Ross leaned back in his chair, still perusing the phone. "Well, lucky for us, it looks like last night's lady has at least a first name. I'll give her a call and see if she can come by the station."

"Who is it?" I questioned.

"Nice try." Detective Ross closed the phone screen—not that I had an opportunity to see it.

"And you're really just going to call and tip her off? Couldn't she be the killer?"

He pursed his lip in thought—or feigning it. Detective Ross was still convinced I was the killer. But he wasn't stupid. He closed his laptop. "Fair point," he conceded.

He stood and gave Felicia a pat on the shoulder. "Let's go pay her a visit. And Mr. Jackson, we'll be seeing you soon."

"Am I, uh, free to go?" I asked, probably a little too skeptically.

"You are. Unless you don't think you should be?"

"No, no," I said hurriedly. "Of course I should."

Ross smirked. "Your grandmother and a lawyer are waiting outside. It'll be a few days before you can go back to your store—or your apartment. And like I said," he added sourly, "we'll be in touch."

6

I spent the next day and a half on house arrest at Memaw's—well, a self-imposed house arrest. It felt like a waiting game, like any moment the police were going to come and knock on her door, then take me to a cell to wait out the remainder of the case.

Memaw, of course, had to hear the whole story. Twice. She told me it took Mr. Grantley, her former boss, a lot of finagling to get me out without the cops making an arrest. But the way Memaw had said it, well, she made it out like that finagling could be moot.

So, I was surprised when Detective Ross called and said I should come pick up my possessions—my laptop and a few other odds and ends from the shop they'd taken with their warrant. He said my apartment and the shop were okayed to go back into my possession, as well.

Briefly, I wondered if it was a trick. I thought it's probably a lot easier to make an arrest when the suspect walks into the station. More than anything, I wanted answers. I knew I didn't kill Ryan Walker. I wanted—no, I needed to know who did. And why.

Neither Detective Ross nor Felicia were available when I picked everything up. So, it looked like that was all the explanation I would get, at least for now. But I did walk out of that place feeling lighter, free. There had to be a reason they returned these things. Perhaps I was no longer a suspect.

The hanging wood sign above the shop was a welcome sight, despite that it was almost noon and the dim neon "Open" sign told its own story. A small bustle of people shopping and eating on Main Street held their gazes on the sign a bit longer than I did. Then their eyes found me.

I unlocked the door and went inside, feeling uncomfortable, wondering what the rest of the town was saying about me, Ryan, and the shop.

Inside, I was surprised at the state the police had left everything. Not that the store or my apartment were immaculate, but neither looked as ransacked as I was expecting. Thinking on it, it made sense—it was probably easier to search for evidence with a structured system and not by tossing everything from drawers to the ground.

There was still some cleaning up to do. I got to it, mostly to busy myself. Also, I hoped to reopen the next day. Not that I thought I'd see a single customer. Ryan's death likely spelled the end for Kapow Koffee, too.

My dream shop... it was over almost as soon as it started.

Of course, a coffee shop wasn't *always* my dream—no kid dreams of brewing coffee for a living. But I drank it often enough, off and on since high school, every day in the Air Force, and every day after. Those first few semesters of college it became an addiction.

Not just a caffeine addiction. I found myself studying up on coffee bean blends and *not* my growing course load.

The Air Force was where I met Gwen. We were engaged.

The plan had been to get out and use our GI Bill to attend Florida State. I would major in business. She wanted to be an engineer. And somewhere down the road, we'd start a firm together. She'd do the engineering, and I'd do all the boring business work. That plan crashed and burned in the first semester—when she met Trevor.

Timing is a funny thing. I'd only spent one semester alone when Pawpaw died, and I moved back to Niilhaasi Bay to keep an eye on Memaw. There was just enough online coursework to not only retain my GI Bill, but also graduate. We opened the shop six months later.

I ran a mop across the floor, trying not to picture Ryan's body lying there. I sighed and let the mop soak in the bucket. I was half out of it, lost in thought, when the bell beneath the door jingled. Before I even looked up, I heard the familiar padding of feet and a loose collar get shaken along with a set of floppy ears.

"Gambit?"

"And friend," Felicia said. She unclasped the dachshund's leash, and he circled the store, probably in a futile effort to search for Ryan. The dog found his usual spot in the faded blue bed beside the display case. He huffed, curling down into it with agitation. I guessed I wasn't the only one with a bad couple of days.

"I kind of figured he could stay with you," Felicia said, "that is, if you're up for it."

I nodded, almost a reflex now. "Yeah, it's fine."

"My daughter begged to keep him. But my hours are crazy, and my folks don't like dogs."

"Daughter?" So, she was definitely a mother.

"Long story. Well, not terribly long. You remember Derek Fox, right?"

"Yeah, of course."

"Remember how we started dating at the end of high school?"

Honestly, it wasn't something I'd thought about often enough that lying in this situation was tough, but I tried anyway. "Wait... You dated Derek?"

"You're not a good liar. You never were. You liked me back then, didn't you?"

I shrugged. "So, what happened with Derek?"

"The usual. Married too young. Divorced just as quick. He gets her every other weekend."

Felicia eased further inside. "Can we talk?" She pointed to a booth—the same one Ryan and crew used for their game.

"Isn't that what we're doing? Talking, that is..."

"I guess some things never do change."

She rolled her eyes and slid into the booth, lounging against the back cushion and the wood partition. If I was exhausted after spending the past two days on edge, Felicia was doubly so. She was again in plainclothes cop attire, but no jacket. Her cream colored shirt wasn't as sharp as the maroon one from the other day. The sleeves and the front were a wrinkled mess. Her hair was down. Curls flowed in all directions.

"Sit," she commanded. "I meant about Ryan—about the case."

"You mean you don't need Detective Ross?"

"Well, not exactly. For now, this'll be off the record."

"Okay," I said slowly. I sat down even slower, skeptical. I still looked outside, thinking Detective Ross might show up any moment.

"I'm off the clock," she laughed and looked down at her watch, "for at least another hour. This case is doing a number on us."

"I bet," I said. "Can I... I mean, am I even allowed to ask what's going on with it? Like, for one, why I guess I'm no longer a suspect..."

"You're definitely allowed to ask, but I'm not obliged to answer."

"It's like that, huh." I felt us fall into a familiar pattern—like the last ten plus years didn't count for anything.

"Yeah, it's like that." She smirked for half a second, then it faded. "I guess you'll probably learn a few things just by questions. And I'll just start with an apology. You won't get this from Ross—and I'm not sure you will from most of the town, either."

We both stared uneasily out the long glass windows to Main Street.

"Kirby, it's just that ninety-nine times out of a hundred the last person to see the victim is the killer. And that knife, well, it made things look a lot worse. You understand, we had no way of knowing..."

"Of knowing what?"

"That it wasn't the murder weapon. The medical examiner barely had to glance at Ryan to tell us that wasn't the case. The knife wasn't in deep, it didn't touch any organs, and there was hardly any blood. In fact, the M.E. said it was luck that the knife was actually stuck in place like it was."

"Then what did—"

"I'm not finished." She put out a hand to stop me from speaking—this really was reminiscent of the Felicia I knew in high school. "See, the time of death is also fishy. We're sure it happened earlier that night. And not here. Of course, the M.E. has to run more tests to be conclusive. But with what we found, we think it happened sometime just after Ryan left Jill Adams' place on the island."

When Felicia saw that the name didn't ring a bell, she said, "Jill Thompson Adams."

"Jill Thompson—like *the* Jill Thompson?"

"Adams, now. But, yes. The very one. She's a nurse at the hospital. He really didn't tell you?"

"A nurse at the hospital has a place on the island?"

"Her ex-husband's a doctor." Felicia saw where my mind was headed. "And he has a rock-solid alibi. He's an OB-GYN. Delivered a set of twins that night by C-section."

"Wow," I exclaimed. "And Jill—is she a suspect?"

"I can't say. But I will say, she looks exactly same as she did in high school. So, if you have a theory on how hundred pound Jill got that body here, I'm all ears."

I shook my head.

"And, obviously, you're out. That is, you're no longer a suspect. At that time of night, it's a twenty minute drive from here and back. There's no record of your car crossing the toll bridge. And why would *you* take a body from the island back here and stick a knife in its back?"

No, I thought, *the only knife I would stick in Ryan's back is a metaphorical one*. I hadn't considered what was going to happen to the comic book side of the shop. But I did give Felicia's words some thought. "Wait... Are you saying someone tried to frame me?"

"And they did a half decent job of it. Ross was ready to book you and close the case. Lucky for you our M.E. thought Niilhaasi was a better place to work than Chicago. Five years ago, when I became a detective, it'd probably be an open and shut case. I'm pretty sure Dr. Doom never looked at the bodies. He just went off what the lead detective told him to say."

"Dr. Doom?"

"A nickname." She smirked again. "Anyway, you're lucky Dr. Capullo's here."

"Yeah... Lucky," I agreed, reeling at the thought that not only had someone murdered Ryan, but they'd tried to frame me in the process.

"Anyway," Felicia took a look at her watch, "I wanted to ask you about those D&D friends. They're an odd bunch, huh?"

"Yeah..."

"I'm guessing there's not, but I have to ask—is there any reason one of them would murder Ryan? I'm asking you because they were all a bit hard to talk to. Granted, Ross made things difficult. You can take the old jock out of sports, but get him around a few nerds and the ego comes out."

I pondered it a moment. "Honestly... I don't think so. But that Damian kid. He did look heated for some reason."

She nodded. "Good to know."

Felicia scooted out of the booth and checked her watch once more. "All right, Kirby, I guess I've got a job to do."

"You want a coffee for the road?" I eyed the espresso machine.

"I would love a coffee for the road," she said, a relieved grin spreading across her face. A familiar dimple on her right cheek sent a flutter down to my stomach.

Her order was simple, a mocha. Before leaving, she took another look around, sighing. "I'm going to see if I can do you a favor. Make sure the town knows you're no longer a suspect."

"Are you going to the paper about the case?" The *Niilhaasi Gazette* wasn't exactly the most reputable local paper, but it was all we had.

"The paper," she said, laughing, "are you kidding? No. It's Wednesday, right? If the chief's secretary, Barbara, hears the scoop, well then she'll tell whoever she sees at church tonight. And by tomorrow morning, the whole town will know it wasn't you."

"Barbara Simone? She's in Memaw's book club."

"Ah, and book club's Thursday. All right, so if not tomorrow, then by Friday morning, the whole town will know it wasn't you."

To my utter surprise, Felicia's plan worked. Thursday morning saw two regulars and a steady trickle of customers. By Friday, things were actually picking up—better than they were before Ryan's murder. Granted, there were some sick individuals who just came in *because* of the murder. Their eyes lingered far too long on the floor.

Adding insult to injury, I lost not only Ryan, but two other staff failed to show up or return my texts and my calls. Luckily, Sarah volunteered to work a double shift. And she was oddly good at understanding Ryan's lack of organization. She not only found the files for his comic book customers but turned a squad of teenage girls onto Ms. Marvel—not to be confused with Captain Marvel whom we'd discussed a few days prior.

"No, see I thought Captain Marvel was badass. Then I read Ms. Marvel," she told me as I frothed milk for a caramel macchiato.

"Ah, I see," I said. "What're you reading next? Batgirl? Wonder Woman?"

She gave me a speculative look, scrunching her eyebrows together. "I can't believe you own this place. No, I don't think I could be a DC fan. I'm thinking of looking into what's what in the Spider-Verse."

"Spider-Man? I've actually read some Spider-Man. Back when the Tobey Maguire movies came out."

"Not Spider-Man per se, but something along those lines. I'll let you know."

"Sounds good." I'd already added the vanilla syrup to the bottom of the cup. I poured in the frothed milk, and dumped two shots of espresso over the top. Next, I haphazardly drizzled caramel over the top until it looked artsy. I put the lid on, ensuring I was the only one who ever saw said art.

"I'll take over from here." Sarah nudged me, which had the effect of directing my eyes to the man standing across from me at the counter.

Marcus Drake, Marc, gave a slight nod toward the booths. "Can we talk?" he asked.

Since high school, my friendship with Marc had dwindled to hardly anything at all. It's strange, but I'd gone from seeing, talking to, and bonding with him daily for over four years to barely "liking" any of his Facebook posts.

Unlike Ryan, who not only maintained relationships but fostered new ones, I let relationships fizzle into obscurity.

Marc sighed grimly—it's a thing, I swear—as I joined him in the most remote booth in the shop, close to the comic display cases and the sleeping dachshund. Gambit had not taken the past two days well. He barely acknowledged me. He wasn't eating. I felt bad for the pup. And part of me thought maybe Marc was here to scoop him up.

"Kirby," he said just as grimly, "I just want to get this off my chest... I know you didn't do it." He sighed like that took off some immense pressure. "It sucks the cops had to arrest you."

"They didn't arrest me," I protested.

"Really?"

"Really."

"Oh," Marc perked up, "well, at least there's that. I thought I heard Felicia arrested you."

"Not exactly... She, uh, took me in for questioning though."

"I bet that was weird." He gave me an odd look; I struggled to figure out its meaning.

"Yeah, it was," I confessed. "But why do *you* say so? Why would it be weird?"

"You know," he shrugged, "because you liked her in high school."

That was a sufficient answer. But I didn't remember confiding that information to Marc. *Ryan*, I thought, gritting my teeth.

"Well, that *and* she liked you..."

"Wait... what?"

Marc laughed through his nose. "Yeah, that was always the big gag in high school. You liked her. She liked you. We used to put you in a room alone together to see if anything would happen. Spoiler alert—nothing ever did."

"Cause I didn't know she liked me!"

"Yeah—that was part of the gag. It'd have been way less fun to tell you."

I choked on the futile anger piling up inside. There was

no use losing two friends in one week—even if this one deserved it.

"Do you keep up with her at all?" I asked. "What happened after high school?"

"Not really," Marc replied. "She went to FSU with Derek, came back married to him and with a degree in criminal justice, I think. She had a baby not long after, and then they got divorced. That's about all I know."

I nodded.

"So, you think you'll make it to the wake tonight?" Marc asked.

"The wake?"

"Yeah," he shook his head, "Ryan's brother said he doesn't want to do a real funeral. I guess it might be a while before they release the body. He's having Ryan cremated and sent to Detroit later. How messed up is that?"

"Pretty messed up." I shrugged. But from what I knew of Ryan's brother, this wasn't all too surprising. "Are you sure I'm invited to this wake? If his brother doesn't think I did it —which he might—I bet he still blames me."

Marc shook his head. "Don't worry about that. It's at Sky Bar. And pretty much the whole town's invited."

"Really? Who invited 'em?"

Marc grinned at me mischievously. "I did… You know it's what Ryan would've wanted."

There was no questioning that.

"Okay, I'll think about it," I said. But I was already thinking about a lot of things—like who framed me and why Ryan was killed. "Marc, can I ask about the other night? What happened with the game?"

"What? Oh, the game. I'll tell you what I told the cops. Nothing happened. We got finished around 11:00, and we all left together. I watched Ryan lock up the shop. He had Gambit on his leash. He mentioned something about a hot date. Then he got in his car and left."

"His car," I looked instinctively outside. "Where is it?"

"Hmm." Marc grimaced. "I'm not sure. That's a good question."

"Well, I've got one more—"

"Okay, shoot."

"Something was up in that game. That Damian kid, what was his problem? Was it something Ryan did?"

Marc chuckled. "Yes and no. But I don't think it was a murder-worthy offense. We'd cut our last campaign short, so we started this game where we'd left off—all in a tight spot against a troll. Damian thought he could take it. I've never seen something like it before."

"Like what?"

"The kid had rolled a natural one—critical failure. Then, on his saving throw rolled a natural one. And Ryan as Dungeon Master, well, house rules say you die if you roll a critical failure on a saving throw."

"So?" I said. I had a foggy memory from my old D&D days. "Couldn't you guys resurrect him or something?"

"Well, we could've. And this part wasn't Ryan's fault. But Tim thought it'd be funny not to. Made him write up a new character sheet and everything. Then Ryan introduced the new character into the game."

"And that's all he was pissed about?" Marc was right—it didn't sound like a murder-worthy offense.

"Well, that and Ryan took Damian's dice." Marc pointed to the shelf behind the counter with the figures and toys. There was a small handwritten sign I'd failed to notice —*CRITICAL FAILURE DICE $10.*

"That's messed up."

"It's Ryan's sense of humor." Marc chuckled again. "I already miss him, bro."

"Me, too." I sighed.

8

W e closed the shop early, at 6:00, giving me a whole two hours before the wake to go eat at Memaw's. Yes, my Friday night plans had been to eat dinner with my grandmother, and they were only livened up by the addition of a wake.

"How are things at the shop?" she asked, splitting a salmon patty with the prongs of her fork. Memaw was of a generation who learned to cook with ingredients from cans and boxes—adding an egg here or there was all the food prep required. Even with the plethora of local fish available in Niilhaasi, here we were eating something shipped from Alaska.

"Surprisingly good," I answered. "Today was a record day. I think we served fifty mochas alone. I'll have to order more chocolate syrup."

"I'll never understand those mocha drinkers," she scoffed. "A little half and half and some Splenda is all that's required for a good cup. Your Pawpaw always drank it black."

"With a cigarette," we said in unison.

She smiled at the thought of him. We both did. "Any news on your friend's murder?"

"None that I've heard." I wondered if Memaw had put together what Felicia had to spell out for me. That someone tried to frame me.

"It's always the lover." She scooped a fork-full of flakey fish. "That, or the lover's ex."

"The problem is, Ryan seemed to have a few lovers."

"Ooh, maybe one got jealous."

"Maybe." I shrugged. "How was book club last night? I'm guessing this was a topic of conversation."

"The only topic," Memaw said sardonically. "Had I known that, I wouldn't've even read that godforsaken book."

"What book?" I asked skeptically.

"Oh, Gail's on a fantasy kick. You'd know it. We read that Harry Potter. You know, with the wizards."

"Harry Potter's a classic. Why would you call it godforsaken?"

She leveled her gaze on me. "I'm just a bit confused. See, I read it. And it was pretty good. But then I saw it on TV the other night, and I swear it had a whole other plot. Didn't make a lick of sense."

"Well, Memaw, there're seven books."

"Seven?"

"Yeah." I grinned.

"Who knows which one I was watchin'. I think it had that young man I like who played Lee Harvey Oswald in *JFK*. He was a prisoner or something."

"Gary Oldman?" I had to verify that one on IMDB. "Memaw, how do you remember things like that?"

"Oh, you'll understand some day. Some things are easy to remember—or hard to forget. Others, you learn to toss away with the garbage. Speaking of, do you mind taking mine out when you leave? I don't want the salmon to sit there overnight."

"It'd be my honor." I winked.

Sky Bar was down on the harbor by The Fish Camp. It had the same style parking lot, laden with oyster shells. The lot was already brimming with cars. But my old Volkswagen Golf slid easily between two crookedly parked trucks. I was probably the only one of the three drivers who'd know that all three of them ran on diesel. I'd also probably be the only one of the three driving home sober that night.

It wasn't like I'd never tried alcohol. But enlisted in the Air Force, I'd seen too many kids ruin lives and careers because of the stuff. A single beer would do me for the entire evening.

Instead of the smell of good seafood and salt air, like The Fish Camp, when I stepped out of the car my nostrils were greeted with a stale urine-like vibe. Hints of vomit wafted through the air—coming here already felt like a mistake.

Would I be welcome? After all, Ryan was my best friend. And I knew I didn't have a single thing to do with his death. But his brother... Ryan had never liked his older brother all that much. I'd only ever met him once. Oddly enough, it was in a similar circumstance—when Ryan's father died. When his mother died a few years later, I wasn't able to get back to Niilhaasi. But I did send flowers.

I passed the bouncer with ease. I'd been here enough times with Ryan to be a familiar face—no need for I.D. Inside, it wasn't as somber an affair as I'd imagined in my head. There were many faces from high school. A crew of about six were doing shots at the bar while others surrounded the pool tables. They took turns regaling each other with their personal favorite Ryan adventure.

"Remember that time he lost one flip-flop and stumbled home for two miles?" I heard one of them ask.

Marc was locked in a conversation with Ryan's brother, Cody. And when he saw me, Marc motioned me over. I was going to find out sooner rather than later whether Cody approved of my being here.

"You need a beer?" Marc asked.

"I'll get one in a minute," I answered.

"Nah, man. I'm buying. The usual?"

"Sure." I shrugged, half wondering if he really knew my usual drink but also thinking he was a jerk for leaving me here with Cody.

I turned toward Cody to gauge his reaction, realizing only too late that Cody was closer than close. His face was in my face, and he grappled his arms around me, wrapping me in the tightest of bear hugs.

"I just can't believe he's gone..." Cody sobbed into my ear.

"I know. Me, too." I returned the gesture, patting the older man on the back. Cody was over ten years Ryan and my senior. Taller than me, round in the middle, his hair was sprinkled with gray.

He released me, finally, and took a long pull from the Bud Light he was drinking. About that same time, Marc returned with a pint glass full of amber liquid. He either did know my usual drink, or he'd made an awfully good guess. "The red, right?"

I nodded, taking it. Our local brewery, McGoons, made an Irish red ale. It was one of the few craft style beers that Sky Bar had on draft. I took a sip as the foam on top settled.

"To Ryan," Marc offered his own bottle up for us to toast. My glass clinked awkwardly against their bottles.

Marc and I played a game of darts while Cody did the rounds. He didn't know anyone here, so he just barged into the middle of conversations and asked people how they knew Ryan. Most everyone welcomed the drunken man into their conversations with sympathy—losing a brother is difficult even when you're not close.

Tim Grayson, in his usual blue shirt, stopped over to chat with Marc. Inevitably, their conversation turned to D&D, claiming Ryan was one of the best dungeon masters around.

"You know he made his own campaigns?" Tim asked me. "We weren't using the books—not always."

I inferred from their conversation that Damian wasn't old enough to attend tonight. *How convenient*, I thought sourly.

A short while later, I bid Marc and Cody farewell. The night was still plenty young, but not for the Saturday morning barista - i.e. me.

I stepped outside onto the boardwalk. The smell of the ocean was distinctively penetrating, salt and brackish water, in stark contrast to the stale beer and smoke of the bar.

I noticed a small figure walking down near the boats on the marina side away from the bar, away from the parking. It was dimly lit with only the occasional white lamp. Her stature and straight blonde hair gave her away; I knew exactly who that figure was. She stumbled, not drunkenly, but shocked to see me up on the walkway looking down on her.

Then Jill Thompson, or rather, Jill Adams, waved.

9

"I was sort of wondering if you'd be here." Jill pulled me in for a hug. This one was more guarded than the one Cody had offered.

"I wondered the same," I admitted. I took a step back. The faint sound of a boat motor cutting off disrupted the repeated splashing of water lapping against the boats docked in each slip. There was all variety here, fishing boats, small bowriders meant for a few hours of family enjoyment, and the occasional yacht, though the yachts here couldn't match those on the other side of the bay.

"I couldn't go in," Jill said, sniffling and pointing up at the bar. "Everyone thinks I did it—or I'm part of it somehow."

"Funny. They think that about me, too."

Even in the dim light, I saw her eyes narrow. "Kirby Jackson! No, they most definitely do not. That's not how people see you. You were a boy scout in high school, and even more of one now."

"I only made it to cub scout..."

"You know what I mean." She punched my arm. Again, I

was taken aback by how easy it was to find familiar rhythms with someone I hadn't spoken with in ages.

"You really think people would think so badly of you? Homecoming queen, varsity cheerleader, senior class president, I'm sure the list goes on..."

"The list *does* go on," she said with emphasis, "divorcee, batshit crazy—and those're the nice ones."

"Yeah," I replied, "I guess guano crazy doesn't have the same ring to it. And speaking of crazy, were you really seeing Ryan?"

She sighed, throwing her head back toward the star-filled sky. "It was a mistake. Listen, I've only had a couple of relationships since my divorce. The last one was an utter train wreck. I thought why not give Ryan a chance, you know? He came over with his cute little dog who I swear he has trained to remove girls' clothing. I had to fight to keep my shirt on, he kept nipping at my sleeve."

She sighed again. "We drank some wine. But he was the same ol' Ryan, you know? He wanted to stay over, but I sent him on his merry way... Kirby, you have to know I never thought it would end like this."

Her eyes went back toward the bar.

"It's not your fault," I responded instinctively. "Unless... you know something?"

"I told your gal pal and that other cop everything I know."

"My gal pal?" I rolled my eyes. "It's not like Felicia's telling me anything. I just saw her for the first time in over ten years. If you think of anything else—anyone else you think could've done it? Or if you just need someone to talk to, I'm all ears. I want to see this thing get solved. And fast."

"Same here." She stared down at the boardwalk. "Let me get your number, and I'll definitely let you know."

She plugged my cell number into her phone carefully, one digit at a time.

"You want any help back up to the parking lot?" I offered my elbow.

Jill smiled halfheartedly. "No, that's okay. I like it here by the water. It calms me. Plus, they say salt's a cure-all. What's that saying? The cure for anything's sweat, tears, and saltwater?"

I shrugged, not having heard that saying.

"I may go up and get a drink here in a few," she told me. "Have a good night, Kirby."

One last hug.

"Yeah, you, too."

I strolled back up the ramp to the parking lot, and found the Golf still wedged between the more massive trucks. Marc had failed in his attempts to persuade me into having two beers, so even the mild effects of the one I'd consumed had worn off completely. I headed for the shop.

The flat shoreline and the bay were to my left, and the moon was high, reflecting on the almost still water. *Moon Bay*, I thought, smiling—perhaps my first genuine smile in days.

To the right of the road was a small nature preserve, a small brackish bayou that eventually led into the bay. But at this spot, it was used as a nature walk. Memaw and a few other ladies met there on Saturday mornings to get their steps in.

The buzz of a text vibrated in my pocket. But again, from years of Air Force training, I didn't answer it. One ticket on base was enough to instill that in my head. I'd lost my driving privileges for a whole month. The text could wait.

But the idiot driver behind me could not.

What had been distant headlights only a minute before

were now racing toward me. The jerk turned his high beams on. I inched over in my side of the lane in hopes this high school kid, or whoever it was, would pass.

They didn't.

The car barreled toward mine. Its left high beam blinded my driver's side mirror. I accelerated to prevent an impact. My eyes scanned the road—was there anyone else watching this? *Where are all the cops when you need them?* I wanted this jackass pulled over.

Despite the bit of torque the diesel engine allowed, it was still no match for the car behind me. Its front bumper made impact with my rear, and the Golf skidded out of my control. It headed straight for the shallow estuary.

I slammed my foot on the brake and the clutch, begging the car not to roll over. Somehow, the two bumpers were free, and the other car sped off around me. I came to a stop, the wheels sinking in muck, but luckily not yet in the water. I tried to back out, but it only dug the wheels in deeper.

Cursing, I got out of the car.

What the— I tried to piece together what had just happened.

Both the rear lights of the vehicle who'd hit me, and its purring engine, became lost in the distance. I climbed out of the brackish mud and toward the road.

That's when it all clicked. A piece of yellow bumper and broken headlight glass lay scattered across the lane. A vision of Corey Ottley's yellow Corvette popped into my brain.

Another car passed by slowly but didn't stop to help.

I dialed two numbers. The first was Felicia Strong, and the second was for a tow truck.

About five to ten minutes later, a uniformed cop arrived and took my statement. I explained it was a yellow Corvette, and who I thought drove it. He just nodded along, not saying much. But at one point, he asked if I'd been drinking, to which I responded 'yes' but only one beer, to which he responded by asking me to submit to a field sobriety test.

The officer was quite astounded by my ability to recite the ABC's backwards. It was something my Pawpaw had bet me I couldn't do. So, of course, I set out to prove him wrong. And funny enough, after all those years, I hadn't lost it. Not a single letter.

Tommy King, the son of Owen King who owned the only auto collision center in town, showed up with a flatbed tow truck. I knew Tommy. He graduated a grade ahead of us. But like almost everyone in Niilhaasi, he was familiar enough to also know my name on sight. He began the process of pulling the Golf onto the bed of the truck.

The fender had wedged itself into the right front tire. The car was undriveable. Luckily, Felicia pulled up around that time, and she offered me a ride back into town. I explained to her, in more detail than I'd given the first cop, what had happened to cause the crash.

"So, you really think Corey did this?" she asked.

"It makes sense, doesn't it? He was always into Jill. And he came into the shop the other day and gave Ryan grief. Maybe he found out Ryan was dating her... And he just went off."

"Right..." She sounded skeptical. "And then he tries to run you off the road when he's essentially got away scot-free? I don't think I'm buying it."

"I didn't say he's the smartest—"

"But Kirby, he *is* smart. He wrote that app and sold it to Facebook or Google or whatever, right?"

"I don't know," I shrugged, "did he? I guess that explains the Corvette..."

"Do you know how many Corvettes there are over there on the island?"

"A lot," she said before I could answer. "We'll investigate it, but I highly doubt Corey did this. Probably some kid with daddy issues out to wreck his father's car."

"Yeah? You ever do that?"

"It never went that far." She smirked.

Felicia was a unicorn—one of the few students at Niilhaasi High who lived across the bay. Her parents were rich and lived on the island full time, which was rare. But she had rebelled. In fact, I couldn't say I'd ever been to her house. She'd always come over to mine or we'd met somewhere else in town.

"How are your folks?" I asked.

"They're all right," she said. "My mom keeps Neena while I'm at work. Or, rather, the housekeeper, Rose, does."

She pulled along the angled parking in front of the shop. I made no attempt to get out. I was still anxious and a little on edge, still wondering what would happen with Corey.

Felicia didn't seem in any hurry either. She sighed and said, "Only a couple more hours of work tonight."

I could see where this was headed.

"You want another coffee?" I pointed at the shop.

"I would love one. Half-caff, though."

"You got it."

In my haste, leaving for Memaw's and the wake, I'd forgotten to put on the shop's outside light, so I pulled out my phone to shine on the door and unlock it. That's when I remembered the text I'd let sit for so long, choosing to make phone calls after the accident instead.

It was from Jill. It read: "*I just thought of something. I'll come by your coffee shop in the morning. We need to talk.*"

Felicia waited as I walked Gambit outside. His bladder was full, and he made sure to mark every lamppost, sidewalk bench, and sign post within the quadrant of shops next to Kapow Koffee.

He greeted her affectionately, and she threw the ball for him as I prepared to make her drink.

Making Felicia's coffee, I wondered if I should say anything about the text. Would she rush over to Jill's now to find out the information? It seemed like something a cop on TV would do. But withholding the information, that seemed more like something someone in the wrong would do. And that wasn't me.

Frothing milk is a loud process, so I waited for that to be done before telling her anything.

"I talked to Jill tonight at the wake."

"Is she still a suspect?" Felicia responded mockingly.

"No," I rolled my eyes. "Seriously, why are you giving me so much grief? I just want Ryan's killer found."

"Sorry," she said guiltily. "I'm just getting this from all sides. My mom's given me a new theory, daily. And Ross is still on about you... Not you as a suspect. He just thinks it's funny we're old friends."

"Anyway," I continued, "Jill just texted me. She said she thought of something, and she's going to come by tomorrow to talk to me about it."

"Interesting," Felicia said slowly. "Let me know how that goes."

"You don't have to, uh, be here? Or go speak to her first?" I asked.

"No." Felicia took a sip of her mocha. She grinned with satisfaction. "I have Jill's statement. If she wants to make another one, or if she tells you anything you think I need to hear, then that's a different story. But remember, I have another lead to follow up on."

"Corey," I suggested.

"Yeah, Corey... I'll let you know if anything comes of it."

"Thanks."

Felicia bent down, petted Gambit one last time, and walked out of the shop.

10

On Saturdays, the shop opened a little later—the residents of Niilhaasi feel less rushed to get out of bed, me included. I thought I'd sleep in, at least a little after the late night. Gambit ensured those plans unraveled.

The dog was up and in my face early and not-so-bright. The sun wasn't yet shining. The sky was a faded blue. A mountainous white cloud was building out over the Gulf, meaning a summer thunderstorm would greet us later that afternoon.

Rather than take Gambit on his usual walk around downtown, I opted instead to drag his leash in the direction of Bay Park. A largish park as parks go, it was mostly a shady area for kids to play with a frisbee golf course surrounding it. There were already some players on the links. Gambit barked as a red frisbee streaked over our heads and out of play.

His temperament proved that the dachshund was a creature of habit. I found myself talking to him once again, reassuring the dog that he would have fun. He disagreed but eventually saw things my way, following after me, huffing after the collar had choked him. I was ninety percent sure the huffing was actually a show put on for my benefit. And it did teach me a lesson—never trust a dachshund.

A small, fenced in area beside the playground was reserved for dogs to bark and sniff each other's bottoms. My intentions were good. We were off to a great start. I threw the ball, Gambit chased after it. It was all going so well... until it wasn't. Gambit's inner Napoleon reared his head, deciding a German Shepard didn't meet with his approval. I had to whisk the dog away, back to the shop, before he was killed by the larger animal.

Once there, we found our typical routine, Gambit in his bed while I filled the metallic containers with half and half, cream, and almond milk. I ground and made coffee. And before we knew it, the shop was again full of customers, with the line at the register not dwindling until early afternoon.

I had almost forgotten Jill's promise to swing by when Marc showed up—somehow he managed to time it perfectly. Sarah came in as my relief. And the two of us, Marc and I, found a booth at the corner beside the comics section.

"That was a good time last night," Marc told me as if I hadn't been there at all.

"Yeah... I remember."

"No, no," he waved me off, "*after* you left."

"Yeah?" I tried to sound interested. But really, I wasn't interested at all.

"Yeah, uh," he stumbled over his words, "Jill Thompson came by. We did some shots. You remember Jill, right?"

Now I was interested. And I wondered how clueless Marc was. Had he not heard who Ryan had been with *right* before his death? Was Marc really that dense, or was he just uninterested in the case?

"I remember Jill," I said shortly. "And isn't it Jill Adams now?"

"Yeah, that's right. But she's divorced. It might as well be Thompson again." He sat there contemplative, obviously remembering back to the day he had sold Ryan and me out —the day Corey Ottley hit Ryan instead of me. Now it seemed Corey had done a whole lot worse to both of us.

"So, what was so fun?" I asked.

Marc shrugged. "It was just a good time. Tim and I ended the night back at Mo's Hideaway. They're open until 2:00 on Fridays. Slices as big as your head."

Mo's Hideaway was the local pizzeria—the perfect crust plus a cheese to red sauce ratio that is so spot on it's criminal. Just thinking about it, combined with it being the lunch hour, made my stomach do somersaults.

"Did Jill go with you?" I asked, trying to sound disinterested. Maybe a hangover explained why she'd yet to show.

"Oh, no," Marc shook his head as if I'd asked the wrong question. "She left well before that."

Then why hadn't she shown?

I wondered if Marc was here for a reason, or was he just here to tell me how much fun I'd missed? The latter wouldn't surprise me a bit. And as far as I knew, Marc had yet to order a coffee. Ever. And I knew his comics folder was empty.

"Anyway," he said, "I heard about last night. Your car accident."

"Accident? It wasn't an accident."

"Oh, whatever you want to call it." He waved me off again. "But that's not it. I heard they took Corey in for questioning."

Marc smiled—he actually smiled. "What an idiot," he said, the grin growing broader. "I've always known the dude can't hold his booze. But I never thought he'd do something *that* idiotic."

Like try to kill me? I wondered. But Marc hadn't put together all the pieces. And I wasn't ready to tell Marc about Corey's connection with Ryan's murder. I'd wait and let the paper, or more likely, the Niilhaasi rumor mill do its job.

"Yeah," I agreed halfheartedly, hoping to find my way out of the conversation and to lunch.

"There's just one thing I don't get," Marc said. "I could swear he left a good while after you did."

"You mean, he was at the wake?" This was news to me.

"Of course he was." Marc looked at me skeptically. "The whole town was there. In fact, I remember, he was talking to that girl Robin while we were playing darts. You know Robin, the one Ryan was, ya know—"

"I know," I cut him off.

I set off toward Mo's Hideaway pondering things. Luckily, the hideaway was just a short jaunt away, walkable. It wasn't necessarily a hideaway, but it was on a less traveled thoroughfare, and its outside seating took most of the space of what had once been an alley. It was now closed off on the other end.

I bought a slice and made one of the worn picnic tables my own.

So, Robin Snider was at the wake, too, I thought, tearing a strand of melted cheese from between my chin and the slice. At least her intentions were noble, or partially so—she'd just lost a lover after all, or a recent lover.

Corey on the other hand... Well, I couldn't believe how brash he'd been even to show up. I wondered, what had driven him to the edge? Killing Ryan, attempting to set me up... At least it was over. Relief that he was in police custody washed over me.

I walked back to the shop, ready to put it all behind me. It was time to figure out how to run Kapow Koffee without Ryan. I wasn't going to lie, not even to myself, a small part of me wanted to cut the comics side—to focus on coffee. But it just didn't feel right, not now. I was going to make this work. Even if it killed me.

Sarah kindly showed me how the ordering system worked—how she even knew was beyond me. But her shift ended far too soon, and one of the quitters, Jason, came in to help with the last shift. He had begged for his job back. And by begged, I mean he asked, saying that he'd assumed the wrong things, and that he was sorry about Ryan.

I was still at least two staff short of where I'd like to be, and Sarah had essentially become assistant manager without the title or pay increase, things I would soon rectify. But it was a short-term solution. When summer ended, I couldn't count on her to stay. I moved hiring up on my ever-growing list of things to do.

That night, I stayed in with Gambit. Without a car, there was nowhere much to go. The nightlife on Main Street was nonexistent as people preferred to be closer to the bay to eat, drink, and be merry.

The dog and I had found some semblance of a routine, a pattern of me feeding him and him claiming every piece of furniture as his own. He liked to sleep in the middle of the bed, under the covers. He made funny noises when he dreamed. And he grunted when landing from a jump off the bed.

But there was something truly special about Gambit, something so hidden, I couldn't figure out what it was. I just liked him. We bonded more and more each day.

To my amazement, on Sunday, the dog finally allowed me to get some rest. We were both roused late in the morning to knocking on the store's front door. The shop was closed. No Ryan, and lack of staff, demanded at least one day of rest.

I hoped this patron would read the sign and leave. I gave them a few minutes to do so before grudgingly getting out of bed, slipping on some clothes, and making my way downstairs.

To my surprise, Felicia Strong stood outside the shop. And holding her hand looking up at her was a young girl who had to be her daughter. The girl looked like her mini-me, the same curly brown hair, dark eyes, the same slender nose.

I unlocked the door, smiling, and allowed them inside.

"You're closed on Sunday?" She sounded heartbroken.

"New hours," I chuckled, "but I'm happy to make you a mocha. What about for you?" I asked her little girl. "Hot chocolate?"

Felicia's daughter was immediately transfixed by the dog. And Gambit, ever aware of the situation—especially when it went in his favor—retrieved his faded yellow tennis ball. He was ready to play.

The little girl looked up at me. "No," she said, "that's okay. I'll have an iced upside-down caramel macchiato, double caramel, and an extra shot of espresso."

"Neena! You will not." Felicia scolded.

"Nana lets me."

Felicia sighed. "My mother takes her to the Starbucks at

the outlets—a forty-five minute drive for coffee. She's six—
she doesn't need the caffeine."

"Plus, it's probably a thousand calories."

"Seriously? Well, maybe she does need it. The girl
doesn't eat."

"I do too!" Neena argued. "I just don't like the food at
your house."

Felicia sighed again. "It's *our* house."

"I really don't mind," I said, inching toward the espresso
machine and out of this mother daughter feud.

"Go ahead," Felicia agreed exasperatedly, then she
joined Neena.

They threw the ball, and the dachshund sprinted back
and forth through the shop. I put both their drinks in to go
cups, made myself a double shot of espresso, and joined
them on the floor.

"So, is this purely a coffee visit?" I asked. "I heard you
apprehended Corey."

"Yeah, *they* did," Felicia emphasized the fact she wasn't
involved with it. "It's purely a traffic incident right now. They
found some damage to his vehicle in line with your accident
and brought him up on reckless driving charges. I'm sure
you'll get a call today from one of the unis about additional
charges that you can press."

"Okay. But what about the murder?"

"The murder?" she exclaimed. "Kirby, there's nothing
that ties Corey to the murder. A crush in high school and a
traffic accident aren't much to go on—"

"Come on," I countered. "You know it was more than a
crush. There's more to this, I'm sure. He did it! *And* he tried
to pin it on me."

"Kirby, that's my job to figure out. And I just don't see it
that way. I think it's best you stick to selling coffee."

"Sure," I agreed grudgingly.

"Whatever happened with Jill?" Felicia asked. "Anything come of your little rendezvous?"

"She never showed up yesterday." I pursed my lips in agitation. "I figure maybe she got cold feet."

"Maybe." Felicia nodded. When she saw my imploring look, she said, "I'll look into it. Or I'll try. But if she doesn't want to talk, I can't make her. Understood?"

"Understood."

We sat there playing ball with Gambit for a few more minutes in silence. Neena enjoyed her drink—or seemed to.

"Hey, Kirby," Felicia finally said, giving the ball a nice bouncy throw, "you were in the Air Force, right?"

I bobbed my head once, wondering where this was headed.

"Listen, I joined a new gym last week. Maybe you'd be interested. You did P.T. in the Air Force, right?"

"We did," I said slowly, "but only twice a week. It's not exactly like the Marines or the Army."

"Oh," she said with disappointment. "Well, this stuff's a bit intense. It's called CrossFit. The owner, Rob, is looking for new members. There's a class pretty early, before the shop opens, if you're interested."

"Like tomorrow?"

She rolled her eyes. "Like every weekday. I'll be there tomorrow. I can introduce you."

"I'll think about it," I said. "Where exactly is this place?"

"You know the movers and self-storage place on the edge of town—Richards' Heavy Lifting?" I nodded. "Well, it's Rob Richards; he runs it from one of the units."

"Interesting," I said, not truly as interested as I sounded. What I meant was more akin to "that sounds awful." Even without the sun up in the morning, Florida was a humid sweat lodge. I knew that place didn't have air-conditioned units—it was one of my parent's gripes when they'd moved to Costa Rica.

But as I watched Felicia and Neena leave, I did think about it. I thought a lot about it. A lot a lot. The idea of seeing Felicia more regularly, and in workout clothes, not in her suit with a badge on her belt. Well, it made the decision easy. The workout the next morning? Not so much.

11

"Great workout," I said through heaving breaths.

Felicia's cheeks were flushed, her brow beaded with sweat, but she was barely winded. She waved at me, grabbed a gym towel from her workout bag, and dragged it across her forehead. "Pretty good for your first day," she told me.

It was a lie. In no way was that workout good for me or for anyone. I felt like I was going to pass out. I wanted to curl myself into a ball and lie on the floor for a while. Everyone was faster than me. They lifted more weight—Felicia exactly twice as much weight as me. I'd never seen cardio combined with weightlifting before. I thought they were two separate events—first, you lift, then you walk on a treadmill or something.

Well, not at CrossFit.

The box—what the members called the gym—was just that, a box. Rob used one of his larger storage units to store the equipment and host the class. And there were no treadmills, stair climbers, none of that. Instead, I found multipurpose power racks, meant for squatting, bench press, or other lifts, with pull-up bars atop them. Despite these racks, the barbells we had to lift from the floor and get over our head. There were rowing machines, and a few heavy-duty tires—the size used on a monster truck—except these were for flipping.

I also found out Rob was the husband of Jen from Jenny's Scrapbooking, the store next-door to mine. Rob was lean with a waist the size of my neck and arms the size of my legs. His own legs, though, were thick and round. He taught the class sipping from a protein shake that looked like a concoction of coffee with something like chocolate chips settled on the bottom.

As we exited toward her car, the sun was peeking through the bottom of the pine trees. I'd had to text Felicia on her personal number for the first time, and ask for a ride. It'd be days before I could pick up the Golf. Dusty said they had to special order a part, which wasn't all that surprising. The closest Volkswagen dealership was over a hundred miles away.

So, I fell into Felicia's unmarked police car, still a bit winded, and cognizant of the smell—or rather, my smell.

"I tried calling Jill last night, texted a couple times, too." It was an odd way to start, or finish, a conversation. Sort of abrupt and in the middle.

But Felicia was tracking.

"I tried, too," she admitted. "In fact, I called up to the hospital. She missed her shift last night."

"Really?" I couldn't tell if my heart was beating faster, or if this was normal because of the working out. Either way, it rumbled in my chest.

"It doesn't necessarily mean anything. People miss work all the time." She hesitated. "They did say this was a first— she didn't even call in sick. Just a no show."

"So, is she missing?" I asked. "Do I have to wait twenty-four hours or something?"

"We don't know that she's missing. She could be at home, not returning calls. But anyway," Felicia tucked some unruly curls behind her ear, pulling into one of the parking spaces in front of the shop, "there's no waiting period. So, if *someone* were to think that she's missing, all they have to do is report it."

"Are you saying I should go check—"

"I'm not *saying* anything."

"It sounded a lot like you said I should go check."

"Kirby, you do you," Felicia said. "If that's what you want to do, do it. But be safe. We still haven't found the killer."

"You mean you haven't apprehended him." I replied cynically. "Don't worry, I'll be on the lookout for Corvettes."

"All right," she said again, sighing. Then I shut the door of her unmarked Impala.

The shop was open fifteen minutes later, or fifteen minutes late—there was no one there that early to judge.

As Mondays typically went, a steady trickle of customers turned to a flood by early afternoon. Back to work and fighting their weekend hangovers, everyone was in need of their caffeine fix.

Sarah took over as barista while Jason took over at cashier, and I was freed to go check on Jill. This after having to non-discretely ask Marc where she lived.

I took a ride share via HytchHiker, which was similar to all the other ride sharing apps. Only a handful of drivers lit up the screen. Like everything in Niilhaasi, the offerings were small. A kid named Neil pulled up in a silver Prius.

And by kid, I mean he looked around the same age as Sarah, so in college, or just out of high school. Mousy hair twisted around his wide oval face. He was nice enough. The car was clean. He even offered me a bottled water.

"I'm good, thanks."

"Suit yourself." Neil did a half shrug and put the car into drive. "No one ever takes the water."

"Really? No one?" I was honestly curious. Niilhaasi wasn't a hotbed of activity. "How many rides do you get in a day?"

I thought maybe Neil saw more action on Gaiman Island.

"Honestly?" he said. "You're my first hiker since, uh, last Monday night."

"A week ago?" I said quickly.

"Yeah, I guess it *has* been a week. It's not like I'm always out looking for rides though. I usually flip it on when I'm out and about—I was just headed to Publix when you put out a thumb."

The app lingo was distractingly funny, but my mind was focused on the date. The last time this kid had shared a ride just so happened to be the night Ryan was murdered.

Could it possibly be a coincidence?

"And where were you headed the other night? I mean, last week, when you had the other, uh, hiker?"

"Oh, man, it was late. I work my other job out at the outlets, and we don't close until midnight. Got to *milk* those tourists for all they got in the summer." He rubbed his fingers together in a mocking gesture. "It's funny, milk, because I work at Starbucks."

"Well, it's less funny when you have to explain the joke," I joked.

"Yeah, you're right," he conceded. "I just hate the tourists, ya know?"

I shrugged. Tourists helped our economy. That was business 101.

"Well, anyway, you'll probably think this is lame, but I went to one of my coworker's houses." He gave me an odd look. "I know what you're thinking, but it's a dude. And no no, I'm not like that either. We just had a beer and played XBox. So, it was fairly late when I drove back here. I think I just had the app on because of habit."

Neil talked with his hands. And the car swerved with each motion. Not an ideal thing when going over a bridge. To one side there were oncoming cars, to the other, my side, a concrete barrier and murky water.

"In fact," he continued, "the dude I drove that night had to be a tourist, too. Wanted a lift all the way over here to the island from around Main. Just like you."

"Really, from Main?" I asked.

"Yeah." Neil nodded. "Just like you," he said again, "over close to that comic shop."

My comic book shop.

My heart began to beat as hard as it had that morning.

My heartbeat only grew faster as I walked up to Jill's front door. The house was nice but smaller than most in the area. Like the others, the house was on stilts. The first floor served as a makeshift carport. It was mildly disconcerting that there was no car parked there.

The siding was shiplap, canary yellow. Both were common enough—there was an almost identical home merely three doors down.

I'd asked Neil to wait at the end of the driveway. I couldn't hear his car engine running. *Damn Prius*. I had to check to ensure he was still parked. This definitely seemed like it was going to be a short trip.

I knocked. I rang the doorbell.

Nothing. No sounds came from inside.

"Jill," I called, banging on the door a little harder this time. I tried calling her, fully expecting to hear her ringer on the other side.

But, nothing.

Sighing, I readied to leave. Maybe Jill had popped out to get something, or more likely, she'd left town. She knew something—I'd convinced myself of that. And I was desperate to know what that was.

I took the stairs down by two, but stopped when I heard it. The sound of cars driving fast into the neighborhood. When the first took the turn in on Jill's street, my heart skipped a beat—it was having a rough day.

Felicia's green Impala skidded to a stop behind Neil's Prius.

Felicia jumped out, and my hands instinctively went up. "She's not here," I announced.

Detective Ross slung the passenger side door out, and he exited the vehicle slowly, stretching, allowing Felicia enough time to put herself between us.

Then Felicia whispered soft enough that only I could hear, "I know she's not here, Kirby. Her body just washed up by Mattonie Point."

12

Detective Ross tapped the top of Neil's Prius. A satisfied grin washed over the detective's already smug face.

"Have a good day, kid," he told the driver. "We'll take good care of Mr. Jackson from here. I promise."

Again, I sat in the *back* of Felicia's unmarked car, when only this morning I'd sat in the front seat with the ability to open my own door.

"Come on. You know I had nothing to do with this."

Felicia adjusted the rearview mirror to look at me. "I briefed Alex on the way over," she said. "Kirby, he knows that I sort of steered you in this direction. It's not that you were here, per se, but from what we've gathered, you were one of the last people to see Mrs. Adams alive."

Mrs. Adams? It flustered me how easy Felicia switched into cop mode. We knew Jill. We grew up with Jill. That wasn't even her maiden name. Labeling her Mrs. Adams, or the deceased—like they did with Ryan—it felt wrong.

"I might be *one* of the last," I said. "But I wasn't *the* last. Remember, Marc said she went into Sky Bar and did shots.

And then she texted me, right before Corey Ottley forced me off the road."

"Speaking of," Detective Ross lowered himself into the passenger seat, "I'm going need your phone for a bit."

"Don't you need like a warrant for that?"

"I could probably get one." Ross smiled.

"Fine, you can have it," I said through gritted teeth.

Pleasing Detective Ross was all but impossible. He wasn't friendly. And for whatever reason, he didn't like me. At the station though, he did eventually relent, at least treating me like an actual person, knowing there was no way I had anything to do with Jill's or Ryan's death.

But I really had no other information to give the detectives. I told them what Jill had said on the dock, then about her text that night, which Ross saw while perusing my phone. Jill hadn't shown the next day to divulge anything further.

"If you think of anything else, you call us." Ross handed me back the phone. "No more of this investigation. I don't care that Detective Strong led you into that direction. If I see you at a crime scene again, *I'm* charging you with obstruction."

Felicia just sat there tightlipped, allowing Ross to speak. She put her hand on my shoulder as we exited the room, but just as quickly the hand was gone. *A momentary lapse in judgment?* Maybe. But the notions Marc had placed in my head were still nagging on me. Felicia had liked me in high school. *Liked me, liked me.* God, even my innermost thoughts sounded like a teenage girl.

It was just that after everything with Gwen, I wasn't eager to find someone new. All the dates I'd been on were set up by Ryan, or one time, Memaw. Those women were nice. But the thought of starting over, of learning someone new, was daunting.

Felicia wasn't someone new. Sure, she'd changed in the past ten years. But only enough for me to take notice. She was everything I wanted.

I exited the police station for the second time in a week. The feeling of freedom washed over me—along with the humid air. I didn't want this to become a habit.

Once outside, I realized I didn't have a ride back. And I *did* have a date that night. I texted Felicia, this time on her personal cell.

Felicia came out of the police station shaking her head, and thankfully, without Detective Ross. She was going to drive me over to Memaw's for dinner.

"Would you mind if we, uh, picked up Gambit?" I asked hesitantly. The day hadn't gone to plan. I was supposed to be back at the shop a whole lot sooner. But I'd texted Sarah, explaining. Well, explaining the best I could. The text had read like this: *I'm at the police station. Yes, again. But I'm just helping out. I'll be back tonight.*

"What am I? Your chauffeur now?" Felicia joked. "And when is it you get your car back, again?"

"Sometime in the next day or so." I shrugged. "I'll just use that HytchHiker app to get around town if I need to."

"That's the silly one, right? The less reputable Uber."

"Right. Anyone can be a driver or a passenger. They don't keep records. It's a flat rate per ride. Then the actual cost is purely agreed upon between the driver and rider."

"How much was your drive this morning, over to the island?"

"More than I wanted to pay," I admitted. "But that kid was nice enough." My memory was jogged. "Hey... So, he did tell me something interesting—the driver, that is."

"Interesting? Interesting how?"

"Something pertaining to the case. To Ryan's murder." I hesitated before saying anymore. I was already getting used to Felicia shooting each and every one of my crime solving ideas down. But she encouraged me to go on. "He said he had a hiker that night. Late, late enough it *could* be our killer. He picked the guy up close to the shop."

I waited for the inevitable response. Kirby, you're reading too much into this. So I was surprised when she said, "Could be..."

"Listen. I know what you're going to say," I said. "It could just be someone who needed a ride..."

"No." Felicia shook her head. "I think you might be onto something—I really do. This *is* Niilhaasi after all. Who'd be needing a ride from Main Street at that time of night? Everything's buttoned up."

I let her sit with the information, to stew with it while I ran inside to pick up Gambit.

Sarah was closing the shop. She gave me a death stare. "You owe me."

"I do. I'm sorry." I knew she meant more than money. But I owed her a raise. "We'll talk tomorrow, okay?"

She nodded.

I ran back out to the waiting car, Gambit in hand. The dachshund scurried across the seat and greeted Felicia. It seemed his one night with her had been enough to bond them for life. His tongue somehow found the inside of her nostrils.

She giggled and pushed him away.

It was a short drive from the shop. We mostly sat in silence, no radio, just the occasional police chatter across the CB.

"I'm missing something," she finally said. "I just don't know what."

She exhaled hard as she threw the car into park on Memaw's dirt track of a driveway. And for the first time, I saw through her facade—perhaps because she was allowing me to. At first, I thought Felicia was just struggling through the problem. Then a tear rolled down Felicia's cheek. Then another. The case had spun into something more than either of us could handle emotionally.

"Jill," she sobbed. "I can't believe it was Jill this morning."

I unbuckled and went in for one of the more awkward hugs of my life across the front seat of a police car. While it was an Impala, it still had all the additional accoutrements of any standard police car. She cried into my shoulder for a minute. Then, like a switch, cop mode was turned back on. Drying her tears with a crisply starched sleeve, she turned to me, red eyes and all. "Kirby," she said, "I can't tell you exactly what happened, but it wasn't suicide. She didn't do this to herself."

I'd already gathered this, but I nodded anyway. I thought of Corey. In my head, I'd already pinned this on him as well.

But every time I put it together, things didn't add up. Corey would've needed to be in two places at once, or so it seemed. He tailed me from the parking lot and sped off toward the island... Unless he went back, which Marc never indicated, Corey wasn't Jill's killer. He might not be Ryan's either...

And if he wasn't? Then who was?

My fingertips rested on the handle of the door. I gave Felicia my best halfhearted smile, pushing it open gingerly.

"Kirby... We're gonna find this guy."

The word *guy* sounded strangely off. I cocked my head in contemplation.

"That's it!" I roared, unable to hold back the excitement of piecing together the clues. "There's something else I forgot to tell you. Marc said Robin Snider was at the wake. It was her—I'd bet anything."

13

"I don't buy it. Did Felicia say what this Robin girl's alibi is?" Memaw asked.

She looked up at me, micromanaging my replacement of her bathroom lightbulbs. I twisted another from the fixture above my head.

Gambit must've also thought I needed an extra pair of paws. That or he was truly starting to take a liking to me. He'd followed us both into the cramped room after sniffing around the house.

"You know she didn't." I gave Memaw a look.

And she gave me one right back. "I'm hoping she'll open up. She's your friend after all. It's not like you'll tell anyone."

"Yeah. Sure. Not like I'll tell anyone. Well, except you. And not like you'd tell anyone..."

I let that sit with her. Memaw wasn't *the* town gossip. But she was *a* town gossip. I handed her the spent bulb and she handed me the replacement.

"How long have some of these been out?" I asked her.

"Well... A few have been out a while. And the last one went out the other day. You know I don't like heights."

"The other day? Memaw! This stepladder is two feet high. How've you been showering?" Memaw's house only had one and a half baths.

"Oh, I don't smell that bad, do I?"

"Memaw!" I said again. "You should've called me."

"Oh, I know you're busy. But this *is* part of the reason I asked you over for dinner." She sniffed at her armpit self-consciously.

I almost didn't notice it, a mischievous gleam in her eye, a look Memaw reserved for being coy. I'd hardly seen her use it since Pawpaw's passing. And usually it had been reserved for when she'd spent *his* money on something he wouldn't approve of.

Yet there it was.

"Part of the reason?" I asked skeptically in an ode to Pawpaw voice.

"Now, don't be mad with me," she started. What she didn't know was it was impossible for me to be mad with her. She was Memaw and that meant something—that is, everything.

"I invited Barbara over," she said. "Her niece just moved here. And she doesn't know anyone. I thought maybe..."

"You thought maybe you'd introduce us?"

"Right. Exactly." Memaw nodded. A curl of an unashamed wanna-be-cupid meddling found its way to her lips.

No, I wasn't mad *with* Memaw. I was mad at the situation. The one she'd put me in.

Memaw showered while I went around the rest of the house replacing more lightbulbs. Then I set the table for four. It'd been a long time since the table had seen that number. I was reminded to call my mom and dad. Last week's excitement had of course found its way to Facebook, and I'd already "missed" several calls.

The smell of pot roast simmering in the crock pot wafted throughout the house. Gambit wasn't the only one with his mouth watering. I set a bowl of water down for him and found him a snack of baby carrots.

Ryan used to keep treats in his pockets the way my Pawpaw had kept change in his. I needed to work out a similar system.

Half an hour later, the doorbell rang. Mrs. Simone, Barb to her friends, looked as she always did—like she was just coming from church. She wore a dress. Her short dyed-black hair was straightened and perfect. Oval wire-framed spectacles sat at the tip of her button nose. She was displeased when Gambit bounded over for a sniff at her ankles.

"Does he bite?" she asked.

"I, uh, I don't think so…"

"No, I think he bit me." She rubbed at her ankle.

"It's just his nose," I said, pulling the dog back. There *might* have been a nip in there. But I couldn't let Barbara Simone think that or Gambit would be touted as the town mongrel who'd almost bit off her leg.

Mrs. Simone ushered herself inside about as far away from the dachshund as she could manage. Then her niece inched forward shyly. She squatted down, just inside the doorframe, and put her hand out for Gambit to sniff.

But the dog felt no need to sniff. He nuzzled his head beneath her hand in an attempt to get a scratch on the ears. He was rewarded handsomely.

Barb Simone's niece was one of the most beautiful girls

I'd seen in my life. And I just stood there, awkwardly staring with my mouth open.

She was brunette, which I'd come to understand as my type. Her eyes were the same honey brown as her hair. Like me, she wasn't aware of the occasion. That is, she wasn't aware we were being set up. She wore shorts and flip-flops. She wasn't wearing noticeable makeup, and her hair was tied back lazily in a ponytail.

"I'm Avett," she introduced herself. She stuck out her hand for me to shake but maneuvered the other one to take its place behind Gambit's ear.

"Kirby," I said. Her hands were soft.

"Kirby is Martha's grandson. He runs the little coffee shop on Main Street."

"The comic book one?" Avett smiled with the question.

"Yeah... The comic book one."

"That's so cute," she said. And she scooped Gambit from the floor, cradling him. His tail wagged furiously.

I couldn't say why I didn't want my coffee shop to be labeled cute. It wasn't necessarily a bad thing. But something about it didn't sit well. I immediately wanted Avett to like me. And cute, I knew all too well, led straight to the friend zone.

Mrs. Simone quickly got me out of this quandary. "It wasn't so cute last week with a dead body lying cold on the floor."

"Oh, that's right," Avett said. "That was your friend, right? I was sorry to hear about that. Did they find who was responsible?"

"Not yet." I shook my head.

"But Kirby thinks he knows who did it." Memaw graced us with her presence. Her hair was still damp. She found a middle-ground between Barb Simone's attire and the casual apparel worn by myself and Avett.

Given the opportunity, they might've called us the younger crowd, but Avett wasn't all that young. She was probably my age, thirty-ish. I wondered if there was a story behind why she moved here. Then, of course, I knew there was—everyone has a story. But was Avett's the cliché? Was she recently divorced and looking for a fresh start in a new place? Or maybe she just graduated from some long grad school program. Maybe she was a doctor or a lawyer.

There was only one way to find out…

14

"Does your grandmother set up all your dates?" Avett asked. We'd just dropped off Barb, and Avett was driving Gambit and me back to the store.

"No. Not all of them," I answered. "Wait... Was this a date?"

Avett smiled—something she did often enough for me to notice the small dimple on the right side of her cheek. She gave me a quick knowing glance before returning her eyes to the road. She knew I liked her. And this was a game. One she played well.

"Maybe not a date exactly," she said. "But *if* we do go on a date, it wouldn't be a blind one. Which, trust me, I've gone on enough blind dates this past year to last a lifetime."

"Really?"

"Well," she clucked her tongue on the roof of her mouth, "some were blind dates—set up by my girlfriends in Atlanta. Others, uh, they were from using an app. I don't care what app it is, the one with the fire, the matchmaker one, whatever—those are blind dates. Not a single guy looked like his profile photo."

"That bad, huh?"

"The worst." She smiled again. I could definitely get used to it. "So, Kirby, tell me how a guy like you is still single. You *are* single, right? Aunt Barb said you were, but I did have a friend back in Atlanta try to set me up with a married man. Granted, she didn't know he was married."

"I'm single," I said. "As single as they come, really. So, I was engaged. It's been just over a year, I guess. It feels like longer, ya know?"

"Yeah. I know exactly what you mean. I'm guessing you're not the one who called it off?"

"No," I answered. "I am. But it was after I came home and found her with someone else. This guy she was supposedly studying with—I don't know if they ever studied."

"Well, they did study *something*," she said sardonically.

"Yeah. Each other." I smiled despite myself. A trace of something painful flashed in my chest but disappeared almost as quickly as it came.

"It wasn't so hard for me to move on," Avett said. "See, I'd been wanting out almost since the day Rick and I got married. He'd only hit me once before then. And we were both drunk that night and being stupid. I thought it was a one-time thing. I was wrong. It was like there was a ratio—the less we had sex the more he hit me. And the more he hit me, the more I wanted out. Sorry, I didn't mean to burden you with my baggage."

"No." I shook my head. "I understand completely. So, whatever happened to him?" I hoped that he was rotting in some prison.

"Oh..." She shook her head in somber reflection. "He went to some counseling or something. He's actually remarried. Still lives in Atlanta. I mean, Atlanta's a big place. You wouldn't think I'd see him around. And I didn't, really. But going to the same stores, the same movie theater, it all just felt wrong. Aunt Barb has always talked this place up. And she found me a job at the hospital."

"At the hospital, really?"

"I'm a nurse," Avett said. "I guess that didn't come up at dinner, did it?"

"No, it didn't," I confirmed. "I think you were too busy laughing about my comic book and coffee shop."

I gestured as we pulled into the spot just outside the front door. The Kapow Koffee sign reflected in the headlight beams. I flashed back to the day when Ryan hung the sign outside. He was so proud of it, of the shop, of this thing we created together.

It was only then I realized I had to keep the comic side open. I wanted to keep a part of him alive.

"I wasn't laughing at your comic book shop," Avett said, laughing. "I said it was cute. Just like you."

My insides squirmed at the compliment. Then everything came into focus—she was talking to Gambit, petting him under his chin and on his proud chest.

When I adjusted and readied to exit the car, Gambit protested. He began to pull at the sleeves of Avett's t-shirt. It was a playful tug, unlike the nip he'd taken at her Aunt Barbara's heels.

"Is he always like this?" she asked. "You're such a cutie."

She buried her face in his, and he licked her lips and nose. Part of me was jealous. Another part, a smarter part, realized the potential here. *Is this how Ryan did it? How he got all those girls?*

"Oh, but the hospital," I said, remembering my train of thought. "You didn't happen to know Jill Adams, did you?"

"Jill," she answered slowly. "Yeah. Well, no... I mean, I knew who she is. Was. I saw her a time or two. I work with her ex-husband. It's on a different floor."

I must've given her a look because she went on, "No, not a chance he would ever be involved. Trust me. Dr. Adams would never—"

"But how long have you known him? A month?"

"About," she said sheepishly.

"Last Monday night, when Ryan was murdered, were you there delivering twins?"

"Yeah. Who told you that?"

"Honestly? I'm friends with the detective working the case. In fact, we were all three friends in high school. I think that's the only reason she's told me anything. Well, that and it happened at our store. I'm sorry to accuse Dr. Adams. I don't even know him. It's just weird, ya know? My friend Ryan was murdered. I don't even think I've said it out loud before now."

"I understand," she said. "But we were there all night. Trust me, it wasn't him."

I nodded. And I was probably looking sullen—because I felt it. If this was a TV movie or something, she would've probably touched my elbow, and maybe we would've kissed. But as it wasn't a movie. She handed me the dog.

And I was left on the curb wondering if I'd already blown it with her.

15

The next afternoon Tommy finally called to say the car was ready. I pulled Sarah aside just after the high school rush.

"Do you mind running the place while I go pick up my car?"

"Not at all." She shook her head. "I think we beat the rush. But I do have some comic book duties to tend to."

She looked at the stack of boxes our UPS driver, Karl, just dropped off.

"Yeah, about that," I said shakily. "Listen, I know you've picked up the slack around here. I've already put in a raise —it'll show on the next paycheck. I'm just not sure what I'll do when you go back to school."

"Wow. That's awesome," she said about the raise. "But there's still plenty of time before school starts back. Don't worry about it for now."

It was easier for her to say. This store was my livelihood. And only last night I'd decided to keep Ryan's side of it going. But I was determined to do that *and* make a profit— something Ryan had been less concerned about.

Sarah looked out into the sea of high schoolers in the booths. She probably expected to see Marc there to pick me up.

"How exactly are you going to get your car?" she asked.

"I'm going to *hytch* a ride," I said jokingly. Saying it, I realized the jokes got old pretty quick. "Oh, and I'm taking Gambit with me. He's been cooped up inside all day."

Sarah nodded in understanding.

I pulled out my phone, tapped into the app, and "stuck out a thumb."

Immediately, a driver on the map turned to converge on my position. I hoped it was Neil from the other day. As far as I could tell he was the closest thing to a clue we had. I wondered if Felicia or Detective Ross had spoken with him.

But it wasn't Neil who pulled up.

An older woman in a less old, but still old, SUV pulled alongside the curb. She was hesitant to let Gambit ride along. But honestly, I was more hesitant for either of us to get inside with her. Maybe Felicia's assessment of Hytch-Hiker was on point. Anyway, this would be my last trip using it.

Once we were to King Auto and Collision Center, I couldn't hop out of the car quick enough. I breathed a sigh of relief as the rickety SUV exited the parking lot, its brakes squealing. But my eyes found the Golf. She looked good— not brand new good, but good nonetheless.

Gambit and I circled around her, then went inside the garage. It was dank and not well lit. It smelled of oil and cigarette smoke.

Tommy King crouched under a yellow car on a lift, a Corvette. It was unmistakably Corey Ottley's. The same car that had caused this whole mess. Seeing it made my blood boil. Tommy caught my eyes and headed over. He wiped his greasy hands on an equally greasy red rag, then stuffed the rag in a pocket.

"Kirby," he said, "how goes it?"

"Better now." I pointed to the car.

"Yeah." He laughed. "It wasn't as bad as it looked. Barely more than the deductible. I'll get the paperwork, and we'll get you squared away."

He led us over to an old worn out desk in the corner of the garage. Or he tried to. Per usual, Gambit was resistant to the leash. He struggled to leave the garage toward a fenced in area at the back where multiple cars sat idle but not idling.

Finally, I managed to yank him over to where Tommy waited. Sitting on the shabby desk was a much nicer laptop. Tommy typed some keys, and a printer behind him began printing. I imagined that was Tommy's contribution to the shop. We were both of an age where the computer almost grew up alongside us. Steve Jobs and Steve Wozniak were just out of their garage when we were born. Our teenage years were spent on AOL Instant Messenger. Tommy grabbed the stack of paper and handed it over.

"This lists all we did and the cost of each with labor. But like I said, the deductible's all you have to pay. Will that be cash or card?"

"Card."

With my keys in hand, all was feeling right with the world. Or at least better than it had the past couple of days— scratch that, weeks.

But the feeling came to a skidding halt when Marc's

black Honda pulled into the parking lot and Corey popped out of the passenger side door.

"Thanks again, bro," I heard him say to Marc, still not registering I was only a few feet away.

It was Gambit's low growl that caught his attention.

Corey looked up wide-eyed. He put his palms up in surrender. "Kirby," he said slowly. He seemed to look for a way around us. There was none. "Dude... I'm so sorry. Are you here picking up your car? Listen. I'll pay for it. No problem."

"Thanks, but I already did." I jingled the keys at him.

He nodded in understanding. "Listen, man. I just want to say thanks for not pressing charges. I don't even know what came over me the other night. Whether it was the booze or... I'm just embarrassed."

You should be, I thought. The thing was—I hadn't pressed charges. I'd honestly thought he had something more coming. Something like the murder of Ryan. I didn't want my frivolous case to hold any of that up. Yet Felicia seemed confident Corey hadn't committed the crime. She probably knew better than me, but I still had my doubts. In my mind, Corey could've killed Ryan. And for all I knew, Jill as well.

Something just wasn't adding up. For me or the detectives. A clue had to be missing.

"You really don't have anything to say to me?" he asked. Gambit was still growling while I'd been lost in my head.

"What do you want me to say? You're welcome? Or better yet, thanks for wrecking my car?"

"No," he shook his head, "I was thinking something more along the lines of what *you* said in high school—the trekkie nerd thing. Maybe something worse. I actually deserve it."

"Why do you deserve it, Corey? Did you kill Ryan? Are you feeling guilty?"

"I *am* feeling guilty," he said. "But that's not it. I didn't kill Ryan. I was just a dick for the last ten years."

"Over ten," I corrected.

"Right... See, you knew Ryan and I both liked Jill. She gave me that one shot. And I blew it. But we'd been pretty good friends ever since. Like, I even went to her wedding. Do you know how hard that was to watch? Hell, I moved back here when she got divorced. I moved just on the off chance that I'd have a chance."

"And did you?"

I stooped down and petted Gambit in attempt to calm him. The fur on the back of his neck was bristled in agitation.

"No, I played it cool. As silly as it sounds, I wanted her to come to me. But she started dating some guy. She wouldn't tell me who it was. I thought maybe it was Ryan. I told her as much, told her about his huge crush on her in high school. But it wasn't him. In fact, when they broke up, she used her newfound knowledge and asked Ryan out herself. Can you believe that?"

"I guess. So that's why you came by that day?"

"I wanted to see if Ryan would shove it in my face. Kinda like I did him when Jill said yes to our date."

"And he didn't."

"Nope. He still wouldn't sell me that toy. But he was honorable. I have to give him that."

"Corey," I said, finally calming the dog enough to think straight, "who was she dating before Ryan?"

Corey shrugged. "She never told me. But I'm with you—I told Felicia as much the other day. We find out who that was, and we've got our killer."

I nodded in agreement.

As I kept the leash taut, Corey sidestepped around us. He gave me a final curt smile before turning to enter the shop. He stopped short, spun on his heels and said, "I am going to pay you back. I'll buy every toy and figure up on display. Whatever it takes."

"Okay," I agreed. "But you still never told me why you hit me in the first place."

"With the car?" He waved me off. "A simple misunderstanding. I tried to talk to Jill on the dock, but she told me she was meeting someone. Then I saw you two talking. I thought it must be you she was waiting for—you hugged her and everything. I was drinking and not in the right state. Marc was still at the bar, and she came in for a bit. Then she left with some other guy. A guy with a boat."

"The killer..."

"Right. I think it's the same guy she was seeing before Ryan. Anyway, Felicia's going to find him. Honestly, I can't wait for all this to be over. I think I'm going to move back to California for a bit. Hell, I've already sold my boat. The house will be easier."

I didn't really blame him. He'd moved back for Jill, and now Jill was gone.

Corey shuffled into the garage. I attempted to head for the Golf. It was finally mine again. But Gambit being Gambit had other plans. He shot toward the fenced lot, almost choking himself on his collar in the process. He had a wheezing fit but still struggled forward.

Then I saw what Gambit was dragging me toward. Ryan's car was sitting there behind the fence, the sun gleaming on its windshield.

16

"Felicia, I said I was sorry. What more do you want?" Detective Ross struggled to keep up as Felicia took long strides toward Ryan's car.

Gambit and I both kept our distance, understanding that something was up between the two detectives. Tommy, who had let us inside the fence, trailed behind us. He held the padlock to the gate in his greasy fingers. He, too, was as interested to know if Ryan's car held any clues to solving the case. He'd told me as much as we waited for the cops to show.

"I'll buy the donuts all next week," Ross said. "Whatever you want..."

"You seriously buy donuts?" I couldn't hold my tongue any longer. "I thought that was just a stereotype."

"It is," Felicia confirmed. "We call it "buying the donuts." It just means he has to buy breakfast."

Detective Ross double-timed to keep up. "Listen," he said. "I understand this is my fault. But it's not as a big a deal as you're making out. You know that."

Felicia turned her head. She gave Ross what we would've deemed in high school as her 'stankeye.'

"You're messing with me, aren't you?" Ross turned back to me, explaining, "I asked some uni's to follow up on the car. And for once, they did their jobs. It was me who made a mistake. I missed the email. Lost sight of it somehow. It was just sitting in my inbox, telling us exactly where to find the car."

"Yeah, someone called the other day," Tommy confirmed.

This was a first. I'd yet to see Detective Ross in such a tizzy. Let alone, him be the one to explain something to me. I was surprised he wasn't embarrassed to act this way in front of me, but he was far more concerned with his partner's attitude.

Of course, I realized now that cops were people too. They made mistakes—even cops as cool and collected as Detective Ross.

Felicia's nostrils flared. It was one of her tells. She *was* really mad. Thankfully, I'd hardly ever seen it directed at me. Only yesterday, she'd said she was missing something. I hoped that this was it—that the car would lead us to Ryan and Jill's killer.

I'd half expected the whole of Niilhaasi PD to converge on the location, similar to when I found Ryan's body. But after I called her, it was only Felicia and Detective Ross that drove up in her green Impala. There wasn't even a forensics unit.

"Trust me," Detective Ross said, his words still aimed at me, "this isn't going to be as exciting as you think it is. Either of you. We're not on *Law and Order: SVU* or whatever it is you like."

"*Castle*," I corrected. "My show is *Castle*."

"Whatever... Wait, is that the one with the guy from *Firefly*?"

"Yeah." I nodded.

"Hmm. I do like him." Ross smiled. He was actually starting to be friendly with me. "Anyway. It won't even be like *Castle*. There's a ninety-nine point nine percent chance that this car holds no additional information. No clues. No nothing."

"You're just trying to weasel your way out of donuts. And if there is something in the car, you're gonna owe more than just that." Felicia unlocked the car with the key fob. Simultaneously, she popped open the truck and said, "But we won't know until we—"

There were several seconds of silence.

"Until we what?" Tommy, trailing just behind me, was the last person to see it.

A large rock, just about double the size of a fist, lay in the middle of Ryan's trunk. It—and the rest of the trunk—was covered in blood.

17

L   ess than thirty minutes later, the parking lot of
     King's Collision was as swarming with police as I'd
     originally thought it would be. Not that Gambit
and I were allowed back anywhere near the car. And this
time, I wasn't being asked into the back of Felicia's Impala. I
stayed because I wanted answers. I wanted to know what
Felicia made of all of this.

She walked over to me, exasperated. But not with me.

"Hey," she said. She leaned up against the Golf. I had the
door open. I was half in, half out. The air conditioner was
blowing cool air which Gambit lapped up, his face to the
vent.

"Hey," I answered. It was a lot like our morning greetings
in high school—back when we got to school fifteen minutes
early just to sit and talk by the statue of a tiger at the
entrance of the school.

"We won't know much until they examine everything,"
Felicia said. "Obviously we think it's Ryan's blood. And we
may get lucky. It looked like there was half a fingerprint on
that rock."

"Only half?"

"Don't worry," she said, grinning. "Half is more than enough. Even half a print is distinguishing enough to identify someone. We just have to hope they're in the database."

"And if they're not?"

"Then I'll do what I do best."

"Pushups?"

She smiled. "Now that you've got your car back, you should come work out again tomorrow. But no. I meant catch criminals. Pushups are like number ten on the list."

"Really, ten? I'll think about it."

Felicia stretched her arms out, sighing. "Yeah. Ross owes more than donuts. We could've really used this information last week. Now we have to play catch up."

"But this all makes sense, doesn't it?"

Felicia eyed me, asking me to go on.

"Well," I said, "the killer used Ryan's car to take the body back to the shop from Jill's—"

"Wait. From Jill's?"

"Yeah. Her driveway was all gravel and sand—nothing that big. But there *is* a stone walkway leading to the porch. All were around that big."

"How'd I miss that?" Felicia said, almost to herself. "So, he took Ryan's car back to Niilhaasi. Then he used that app, HytchHiker, to go back across the bay, and pick up his own car."

"Did you ever talk to that driver, Neil?"

"We did. But he gave a pretty nondescript description if you know what I mean. White male, average height, average build, all that. Dark hair, but Neil said he wasn't really paying attention, and it was pitch black that night. So the guy could be blonde for all we know."

"Maybe the killer drove back over the bay," I offered. "Unless, of course, he lives on the island."

Felicia pursed her lips. "It's a thought... It definitely wouldn't hurt to check those toll logs."

I'd already told her about what Corey had said. But she was at a loss as to who Jill's mystery ex-boyfriend was as well.

"I guess I'll get going," I told her.

She nodded and gave me a tightlipped smile. "Seriously, I better see you tomorrow morning. Exercise is good for the body and mind."

"And maybe you'll know more about that thumbprint?"

"Maybe," she said. "But I probably *should* stop talking to you about the case."

"Tomorrow then." I hoped it was only a threat. My drive to solve this case was equal to hers.

"Tomorrow." She grinned back at me. "It's only a—"

I shut the car door before she could complete the singsong lyric. The diesel engine puffed out a cloud of black smoke, and Felicia waved the exhaust away, sticking out her tongue at me.

It really was beginning to feel a lot like high school.

Sarah was just flipping the placard on the door to closed when Gambit and I returned. The dog padded inside like he owned the place which I guess he sort of did, in a way. After all the excitement of the afternoon, he snuggled under the blanket in his dog bed for a well-deserved nap.

I lingered beside the door while Sarah returned to the counter, picked up her purse, and a stack of new comics— Ryan's lasting effect on her.

"I'm so sorry," I said guiltily.

"Sorry? What for?"

"For leaving you in the lurch... again."

"It's not a problem," she said. "It's not like I have much of a life outside of here anyway."

"Wait. What?" Her words didn't compute. "That's not true. Don't you go to the beach every morning? Isn't that where *your* crowd hangs out?"

Sarah rolled her eyes. "Yeah, I mean folks my age do. But *I* don't have a crowd. I just sit in the sand and read. These are my company." She lifted up the thinly packaged books.

"You're not afraid of ruining them?"

The first time was an eyeroll. This time she was able to see to the back of her head. "Do you know how many comics they print these days?" She could see by my face I didn't. "A lot. Unless it's a variant cover, ya know limited printing, drawn by another artist, then it's probably not going to be worth much in the future. I'm actually doing what nature intended. Reading."

"Okay. Well, enjoy your reading. And, as promised, Friday's the big day. Huge pay increase. Not really. But decent pay increase."

"Looking forward to it." She blew past me, setting the bell on the door to a jingle before I muffled it and locked up.

For the first time in what seemed too long, I was ready for a cozy night alone—well, alone-ish. Gambit scampered up the stairs. Walking up them just wasn't his style, he had to build up to a full sprint, ascending them like he was about to take flight.

"With those floppy ears, you just might," I told him.

He shook them along with the collar in reply.

The studio had just enough space and furniture to be deemed livable. A bed, a TV, and a dresser. The couch was new, hardly used. Besides, it was more comfortable to watch TV from the bed. We settled in for a *Castle* marathon. And I reluctantly set my alarm to make it to CrossFit the next morning.

I'm doing this for the information on the case, I told myself.

"And the exercise," Felicia's voice popped into my head.

Right. And that.

But maybe that wasn't even true either. What was it with this town and old high school flames and crushes? Or does everyone get hung up on the past?

I closed my eyes, my mind still whirring, wondering if I could turn back the sands of time, would it matter? Would Felicia have ended up with me? Or was this our fate all along?

18

The alarm hit me like a ton of bricks the next morning—and I'm not using a metaphor. I yanked the phone from its charger and held it over my face. But like the goof I am, it slipped through my fingers and fell the three or four inches, hitting me squarely in the bridge of my nose.

This is my life, I thought. I wasn't meant for grander things. That dream of Felicia in a white dress was a trick of my subconscious. Though it was me who played the trick, thinking those not-so-subtle thoughts before bed.

I kicked off the sheets and got out of bed, rubbing at the bridge of my nose. I timed it just so I'd get to Richards' Heavy Lifting and Storage at the start of the class, not a second to spare—even for injuries such as this one.

"Are you coming with?" I asked Gambit. The dachshund was under the sheets somewhere. A soft snore gave me his answer.

I rushed down the stairs and out. Even in the predawn, the air was muggy and hot. I arrived at the storage unit in the nick of time—or what I thought was the nick of time.

"If you're on time, you're late." Rob sounded just like an Air Force drill instructor. Looking at him, I guessed he'd probably served as well. *Army or Marines*. He marked a star beside my name on the whiteboard. I had no clue what that meant, so I started the warmup.

Felicia was well into warming up, her brow already glistening with sweat. She gave me a slight smile. "Glad you could make it."

"Body and mind," I reminded Felicia of her own words.

She proceeded to blow through the workout as if it was nothing. She lifted more weight than I could, ran faster, and she could actually do a pull-up—while I struggled, using some sort of rubber band to assist me. With one foot slipped inside the band, I dangled from the bar, barely able to propel my chin all the way up.

At the end of it, I was winded. Sweat pooled on my chest. I lay in a heap on the floor making a sweat angel. Felicia hovered over me. She took a swig of bottled water and said, "You know you're not finished, right?"

"Oh, no. I'm definitely finished."

She smiled mischievously, then pointed at the star beside my name. "You were late."

"Okay..." At this moment in time, all I wanted to do was stare at the storage unit's ceiling.

"It means you have to do twenty burpees," she said slowly.

"Twenty what?"

"Burpees," she answered.

I sat up, and Felicia demonstrated. It was like a pushup on steroids. She lowered herself to the ground in one movement, pushed up, and jumped at the end, clapping her hands over her head.

"Twenty of those?"

She nodded.

What had I gotten myself into?

When the agony of the burpees was over, I was eager to speak to Felicia about the case. She was already to her car by the time I caught up, holding the stitch at my side.

"Hey!" I called to her. "Did you find anything else out? Fingerprints? A car driving back over the bridge? Anything?"

She eyed me wearily, already exhausted by my questions. "You're not going to give this up, are you?"

"Not until it's over."

"We did find something. I'll stop by later, all right?"

"There's a mocha on the house waiting for you."

She smiled and got in her car.

I waited for what seemed like forever for Felicia to show. What exactly did *later* mean? It could've meant ten minutes, an hour—just enough to shower and get ready for work. Or it could be that afternoon...

It was beginning to look like the latter. The store regulars trickled in, and even a couple of irregulars.

Tim Grayson trudged into the shop with Damian in tow. The two were an odd pair, a middle aged man and teenager. Then I realized something. They sort of shared some distinguishing features—bushy eyebrows, wide foreheads, a crook in their noses.

Damian was obviously Tim's son. *How I did I not see that before?*

"Hey, guys. How goes it?" The two were given a genuine Kirby smile, even if Damian's high school angst attitude didn't necessarily deserve it.

"Good morning," Damian said stiffly.

"Good morning." Tim gave his son a look. "We thought we'd come by and show our support now that your name is truly in the clear. I heard they found a new clue yesterday—and it was all down to you."

"No, it was down to Gambit." I gestured to the sleeping dog.

"What about *our* names, Dad?" Damian said under his breath and just loud enough for the whole coffee shop to hear. "He tried to throw us under the bus."

"Now, now. Kirby was just answering the detectives questions. The same as us. Kids..." Tim smiled. "I'd like one of those caramel drinks. And Damian, what would you like?"

"It's called a caramel macchiato. And I just want regular coffee—with room."

"You got it," I told them.

It took only a few minutes to whip up Tim's drink. Damian doctored his *regular* coffee up with sugar packets and half and half until the coffee's coloring was the same as Tim's caramel drizzle.

"Tim," I called, setting down the drink. But I didn't let him leave with it, not yet. "Hey," I said, "I know it might be short notice. But what would you guys think of an impromptu game of D&D this Friday night. Ya know, kind of something in Ryan's honor."

"Oh, there's no such thing as an impromptu campaign."

"Sorry. I just meant we could use my old starter book. I think there're some campaigns in there we could try."

"Dad's got a few of his own making," Damian chimed in. "I mean, if you don't mind him being dungeon master."

"I'd love that. So, does Friday around 9:00 work? I'll see if Marc can make it."

They nodded, grinning. "Sure does. See ya then."

And for half a second my heart felt full and relaxed. I felt good. But only for half a second.

"So, there goes any Friday plans." The voice was a familiar one but new enough for me to do a double take. Standing in line, Avett smiled at me like she'd caught me stealing mom's cookies from the cookie jar. Her classic red lipstick was a stark contrast to her almost too white teeth.

This girl must not drink coffee.

"Yeah... It looks like I just booked Friday up." I hadn't really expected to see or hear from Avett again. I was confident I'd blown it trying to implicate her friend, Jill's ex-husband Dr. Adams, in Ryan's murder. Yet here she was. And despite my utter lack of suave, I had to at least try to ask her out.

"I am pretty free Saturday though," I said, making my way over from the espresso machine to the cash register.

"Saturday... Hmm..." She feigned thought. "What about tonight?"

She was the type of forward a guy as shy as I am needs. "I could make that work," I said confidently.

"Great. I'll see you tonight then!" She turned to leave.

"You don't want to order?" I called to her. "Plus, I don't know where you live."

"I'm not a big coffee drinker," she confessed, turning at the door. "And I'll just meet you here at closing, all right?"

I nodded. "See you then."

19

The rest of the day passed with little else to offer. Felicia never showed. I figured, or hoped, it was because she was wrapped up catching the killer. I kept typing out a text for her but never hit send, figuring she would talk to me when she was ready to do so.

So, a little before 7:00 we swept the floors, wiped down counters and tabletops, and I let Sarah out the front before racing upstairs to shower and change. Two showers in one day wasn't necessarily the best for the environment. But I stank of sweat and coffee grounds—I figured if she didn't drink the coffee, then she probably didn't like the smell either.

A light pair of khakis had to suffice, though I usually only wore them for work in the winter. I put on a button-down shirt and rolled the sleeves. Flip-flops, or slaps, as my dad called them, were the only other shoes I owned besides the tennis shoes I used for workouts. This mashup ensemble was what I deemed date apparel in the Florida summer.

Gambit lunged at the door when Avett arrived. I asked her if it was okay to go on a walk with him first. She agreed, and he did his best to impress her with the number of times he could raise his leg in a quarter-mile. I counted fifteen.

"So where were you thinking of taking me?" she asked. I locked the shop again, this time leaving Gambit inside to roam.

"Technically, didn't you ask me out?"

"I don't like technicalities. But no. You asked about Saturday. I just moved up the date."

We both let go of the fact she originally insinuated about my Friday availability.

"Okay... What do you think about the Fish Camp? It's Thursday, so there might be a crowd. What am I saying—it's any day of the week, it's definitely a packed house."

She sheepishly bowed her head. "I've actually never been. I've never been too big on seafood. I mean, maybe I've added shrimp to a plate at Outback, but real freshly caught seafood isn't something you find very often in Atlanta."

"We're nipping this thing in the bud," I told her. "There's no reason to live here if you don't eat seafood. How has your Aunt Barb let you live here two months without taking you to the Fish Camp?"

She smiled, sheepish this time. "She got in a little kerfuffle with the manager a year or two ago. She's sworn it off."

"That sounds like a deathbed regret if I've ever heard one." She snickered as I opened the Golf's passenger side door for her.

The drive over was a pleasant one. We chitchatted about work and the weather—about how the sweltering Florida heat wreaked havoc on the glands and made most showers utterly moot.

I told her about how I was bound to always smell like coffee, no matter what scented soap I used.

She made a face.

"You really don't like coffee, huh? How do you function? Let alone function as a nurse at the hospital."

"You're going to think it's silly. But I drink a tea. It's called Yerba Mate. I'll be honest. It's a bit of an acquired taste. It's even more bitter than coffee and packs a lot less punch."

"I think I've heard of it," I said. "But we don't carry it. White Tea's the best I've got."

"White Tea's fine in a pinch. See, I'm kind of obsessed with my teeth. My mom says I should've been a dentist."

"Really?"

"Yeah," she nodded, "but there's a difference between my own teeth and those of others."

"I understand completely. Unfortunately, I have the coffee drinker yellow tinge. But I do try to floss, um, weekly."

She laughed. It wasn't a joke.

"I thought you said this place was going to be crowded," Avett said sarcastically. The Golf crunched over oyster shells as we circled the lot two times before finally creeping behind someone and stealing their spot.

After a "short" wait, we were seated on the patio close to where I'd eaten with Memaw the night before Ryan's death. I remembered the looks from Robin and her husband, Scott—both were still prime suspects in my mind. But I let those thoughts escape me as I explained the menu.

"Market price—it sounds expensive," Avett said.

"Not really," I pointed, "it's written on that chalkboard over there. Plus, if I recall, I invited you out, so obviously I'm paying."

"Obviously." She smiled. "Do you bring all your dates here?"

"Yeah. All of them," I said jokingly, implying I didn't date very often—which was true. But I knew better than to tell her the dates I did have were here, and they were mostly with Memaw. On top of that, the old gal hardly ever let me pay.

I ordered amberjack, my go to when cobia's not available. I talked Avett into grouper, a specialty in pecan flour and a honey Worcestershire sauce. It didn't fail to impress. Avett was already talking about her next meal there even before we split a slice of Key lime pie.

"That seals it," she said, flicking her napkin around her still perfectly red lips. "Best meal I've had in ages."

"The most calories I've had in ages." I struggled to get out of my seat, but that was soreness from the morning's workout, which justified a few extra calories, but probably not the pie.

The thought of Felicia briefly popped into my mind. She had never stopped by. And I was sure if they had caught someone, the news would've trickled to me somehow.

"Do you want to walk it off? We can walk down the docks..."

"I'd love that," I answered. Something inside me told me to grab her hand—it told me she wouldn't protest. I did so. Then she made the effort to interlace her fingers with mine.

Who is this girl?

We walked hand in hand, listening to the soft slapping of water against the boats and the pilings. There was everything from fishing and shrimp boats to a yacht and a few dinghies, probably not worth the cost of the slips they were inside.

"That's odd." Avett brought me in closer. She pointed. "All the others say Florida. Look at this one... *Phoenix*," she tested out the name. "From Mountain View, California."

It was a sailboat, probably just a few feet over twenty. But nice enough to live on.

"Oh, I bet that was Corey's. He made it big in Silicon Valley. Then he moved back here. I think he said he sold it, though."

Avett nodded. "Ah, that explains it."

In a perfect moment, she titled her head up toward mine. Her eyes locked, not on my eyes but on my lips instead. Her lips weren't in a smile but parted in a familiar enough way. I knew what I had to do.

I went in ninety percent of the way. She closed in the other ten.

First kisses are hardly ever the stuff of storybooks or what you see in movies but somehow this one was. It wasn't a make out fest, it lasted no more than two whole seconds. Her lips were as soft as I'd been imaging throughout the whole day—ever since that smile at the shop. And when it was over, she pecked my lips one more time before smiling. She led us both down the boardwalk toward the car, her hand still tangled with mine.

Now there's an advantage to owning a shop above where you live—an advantage I hadn't employed until the moment. What the shop did was provide a totally nonthreatening place to be alone with someone without actually being in their home, or in my case the apartment upstairs.

I parked beside Avett's little coupe. We both got out. It looked like we might share one more kiss, underneath the Kapow Koffee sign. But I just wasn't ready to say goodnight just yet, and my hope was that she shared that thought as well.

"Do you want to come in the shop? I'm sure Gambit will be happy to see you..."

Avett pursed her lips.

God, those lips.

"You said you have white tea," she said. "What about chamomile?"

"We definitely have chamomile." I smiled and unlocked the door.

Gambit greeted us, his tail hammering on my shin, as I turned the lights on a dim but bright enough to see setting. It looked like the way it did in the early morning hour—6:30 to 7:30AM when only one customer at a time stops by.

I made us both tea. I decided I didn't want to be up too late, thinking maybe I'd hit CrossFit again the next morning to try and pry information from Felicia. We settled into the same side of a booth. That was actually her choice—I'd sat down first.

I was happy with her choice, and even happier as she scooted in closer to me. I did my best middle school yawn and put my arm around her waist. This was going well. My first date in over a year and it felt like old hat. It felt good.

"So tell me more about you," she said. "Was this shop always your dream? Seriously, I think the comic book thing is growing on me. I really like the vibe in here. It feels like a place you can come and just sit for a while. But I guess maybe it's because we're alone. Does it fill up with geeky kids in the afternoon?"

"No, not really. I think we drastically overestimated the

number of geeky kids that live in Niilhaasi. In fact, it's mostly geeky adults. And they come in just long enough to get their comics and run out the door."

She chuckled.

"Honestly, the comic shop wasn't my idea. My buddy Ryan helped me get this place started. I grew an affinity for coffee when I was in the Air Force. You haven't had bad coffee until you've had Air Force bad coffee. I sort of took it upon myself to right my squadron's wrongs. Then in college I studied at the local Starbucks. I got used to the smell and addicted to the taste."

"Oh, what did you study?"

"Business," I said.

"My ex," she said hesitantly, "that's what he claimed to study. We met in college. It looked more like he studied video games. His bad grades were just the first of many problems. He could never hold down a job for more than six months."

"That's kind of becoming the norm these days, isn't it?" I asked rhetorically.

She nodded.

"Gosh." She sighed. "What are we supposed to talk about if we can't talk about the past? I'm so sorry I keep bringing up my ex. Every time I do my stomach starts twisting on itself. I keep thinking I'm going to blow it with you."

"Really?" I smiled. "I keep thinking the same thing."

She looked at me, worried.

"No," I said squeezing her closer, "not that you're going to blow it. I mean I keep thinking that I'm going to blow it."

She laughed. "I knew what you meant. I was just playing."

She gave me that look again, the one from the docks—the one that told me it was okay to kiss her.

Again, I went ninety percent of the way. But this time Avett didn't go ten. There was no kiss—because the bell on the door jingled. And Felicia walked into the shop.

20

"I am so sorry," Felicia said guiltily.

Avett scooted away from me as if I had the plague, or perhaps more accurately, as if we were teenagers caught making out by her father.

"No, it's okay. I was just getting ready to leave."

"Were you?" Felicia asked.

The same thought occurred to me as well.

Avett scooted out of the booth, almost knocking over her tea. She gathered her purse. "Maybe not," she admitted. Then she gave me a questioning look as I slid out from the booth after her—there's nothing worse than being the only one sitting when everyone else is standing.

"Oh, right... Avett, this is my friend, Felicia. She's a detective with the local police."

"Right." Felicia put her hand out for Avett to shake. "I kind of promised to swing by here with some information, but the day got away from me. I saw the light on when I was passing by and figured Kirby must be inside working. I never thought..."

"You never thought I'd be on a date," I joked.

"Stop. You know what I mean."

Gambit found his way between Felicia's ankles. The dog liked her more than me. She stooped down to scratch behind his ears.

"Well, it was nice meeting you," Avett told her. "And Kirby, I'll talk to you soon, okay?"

"Definitely," I said through my inner protest at her leaving without another kiss. I couldn't tell if I was seeing things or what, but it looked as if there was some jealousy in Avett's eyes.

Who was I kidding? Avett probably didn't care. Felicia either. She had her own things going. This was just one date. *And just one kiss*, my inner monologue said harshly.

"She seems nice," Felicia said kindly. "In fact, she's familiar. Does she work at the hospital?"

"Yeah. With Dr. Adams, Jill's ex."

"That's where I know her from."

Felicia stood and made her way over toward the bar. She eyed the espresso machine longingly.

"You want a mocha?" I asked.

"Half-caff? I actually need to go back in soon."

"Coming right up." I slipped around the counter. "So, what news do you have for me?"

"We caught him," she said matter-of-factly.

I stopped with my finger over the grinder button. The espresso beans were still very much bean.

"I'll tell you all about it *after* coffee is made." She waved me on. "But it's the reason I never made it back until now. It's been a busy day and night, and it probably won't stop until we've got it all pieced together."

I quickly turned on my autopilot latte making skills, completely forgetting she asked for half caffeine.

"Crap," I said. "That's fully loaded. I forgot to use the decaf beans for the other shot of espresso."

Felicia just shrugged and took a sip. "I can probably use it anyway. No way I'm sleeping tonight."

She went over and took a seat in the same booth that Avett and I had just shared. I came over and sat across from her.

"Explain," I implored.

She smiled, shaking her head. "You're cute when you're anxious." She took a long sip of coffee, making me ever more anxious.

"Your tip about the bridge was spot on. That's pretty much how we caught him. Remember Robin Snider?"

I nodded. In my head, Robin was still a suspect.

"Well, she and her husband Scott, they were each other's alibi. Scott had been told that night about Robin's affair with Ryan, but they both swore to have made up. Said they were with each other all that night." She coughed. "In the intimate sort of way."

"Wow," I said.

"I know. You'd be surprised how many times I've heard that as someone's defense."

"How many?" I asked, actually intrigued.

"Just the one—I was kidding."

I laughed. "Okay, so what does that have to do with anything?"

"They were lying. Scott's car passed through the toll that night. And surveillance shows that he was the only one in the car. They weren't at home like they'd said."

"So Scott did it?"

Felicia nodded.

"And Jill?"

She nodded again.

"We think Robin was just trying to protect him. Say that he was home when he wasn't."

"But I don't remember seeing him at the wake," I told Felicia. "I remember seeing Robin there, but not him. I'd remember."

"Were you drinking?"

"I had one beer. And I'd remember Scott. He gave me a pretty evil look the night before Ryan's murder. I saw them both at the Fish Camp, remember? That's probably where she told him about Ryan."

"Probably." Felicia nodded. "So, Kirby, what are you trying to say? Do you think maybe they're covering for each other? Maybe he killed Ryan, and she killed Jill?"

"That's exactly what I'm trying to say."

"Well, that would explain something," Felicia said. I gave her my most questioning face, encouraging her to continue. "When we pressed Scott on how he killed Jill, he never really answered. He'd skip over the murder part and then just say he threw her in the water. You know we've intentionally not told anyone how she was killed for this very reason."

"So, he says he killed her and threw her in the water. Do they even own a boat?"

Felicia rolled her eyes. "It's Niilhaasi—everyone and their mother owns a boat."

"Not me."

She rolled her eyes again. "I'm tracking with you on this. I really am. Just because he confessed doesn't mean he did it. He was even pretty vague about what happened with Ryan. We're waiting to see if that half fingerprint matches up with his."

"What if it doesn't?"

"Well," she shrugged, "he still confessed. Who knows.

Maybe that's your fingerprint. He was trying to frame you after all."

"Did he say that?"

"Not exactly in *those* words."

I nodded, but something about this didn't sit right with me.

"You should really look into Robin," I said. "If it was Scott who killed Ryan, fine, but why would he kill Jill if that was the person he was seeing?"

"Wait! What?" Felicia jerked her cup down to the table. She looked at me as if I'd said something wrong.

"What?" I questioned. "What'd I say?"

"You don't remember the words that literally just came out of your mouth? You said Scott was seeing Jill."

"Right." I nodded. "I was just doing some mental calculations. Ryan told me that not only was Robin having an affair but Scott was too. So they were both going to work it out. Then I told you what Corey said. Jill was just dating someone, someone she wouldn't tell Corey about. Two plus two equals four, right?"

Felicia nodded. "Usually. I didn't know about Scott's affair. That does shed some new light onto the case."

"They never said anything about it?"

She chuckled halfheartedly. "Maybe you don't know how these interrogation things *usually* go. But it's not what you see on TV—on *Castle*," she corrected. "There's always a lawyer present. They answer *some* questions directly but aren't an open book like you were the day you came into the station."

"So what do you think?" I asked.

"I think it's something I have to think about," she confessed. "I'll know more when that fingerprint is analyzed. As it stands, there's nothing that points to Robin killing Jill. As far as I can tell, they'd never met."

I nodded. "I understand."

Felicia stood up. Smoothing out her button-down shirt, she took another swig of coffee. "So, Kirby, your investigation is done now, right? I'm going to handle the rest. Thank you for all the insights. But it's time to play regular citizen until the trial."

"That's me," I said. "Plain ol' citizen."

"Oh, and she was cute," Felicia said, leaving. "Real cute."

Was it me or was there a twinge of jealousy in those words? *It has to be me*, I thought sensibly. There was no way two women would get in a tiff over me.

21

Fridays were typically the busiest day at the shop. I couldn't say exactly what brought the people out in droves. Maybe it was just they were cooped up inside all week long and ready to stretch their legs, although stretching them in the cramped booths at the shop was next to impossible. Karen would try to anyway. But her arrival was at least an or so hour away.

The early morning hours were always mine to do as I pleased with only a random customer here or there. I prepared for the onslaught, making extra of the medium roast coffee, grinding espresso beans early, and making sure the small fridge in the front of the store was stocked with the milk from the industrial size fridge in the back.

I paid only a little mind to the jingle of the bell at the door. I'd already seen two golfers on their way to the links. I finished filling the canister with half and half, set it out, and turned to see the newcomer.

My heart stopped.

"I know what you're thinking," Robin Snider said.

"You're thinking Scott really killed them. And I'm here to defend him."

She obviously didn't know where my head was—because I was thinking, *what is a killer doing in my shop?* I was wondering if there was anything back here for me to defend myself with. The bagel knife was long gone, as were the bagels. I hadn't ordered more since Ryan's death.

If anything, I was going to use that giant Captain America bust Corey was after. But Robin put her hands up in mock surrender. There was nothing in them, no gun, no knife. Nothing.

"That *is* what you're thinking, isn't it?"

"Something like that," I lied slowly. "If that's not it, what are you doing here?"

She bit her lip nervously. "You probably don't remember, but we met a little while back. Around the shop's opening. That's when I met Ryan."

I vaguely recalled that day and nodded. But there was an influx of people that whole week—they had come mostly for the free cup of coffee offered to each new guest in exchange for an email address. I kept meaning to actually use those addresses to send out promotions or just to advertise in general.

"It started off innocently enough," she continued. "He was really sweet. And my marriage was going to shit. Don't get me wrong, Scott's a good person. We've just faded. No kids to tie us down, we just lost our spark, ya know? It isn't his fault. It isn't mine. Well… see, I thought it was mine until he told me he'd been seeing someone else."

Jill, I thought.

Gambit, not really a morning dog, lumbered out of bed. The familiar voice must've roused him. He hopped his two front legs onto Robin's knee and stretched his long back, yawning.

"Hey boy. Long time no see." She gave him an odd pat on the top of his head. I guessed she wasn't really a dog person.

"So he was seeing someone," I prodded.

"Right," she said. "But he never said who."

"I'm sorry," I said, flustered. "What does this have to do with anything? You told him about Ryan, correct?"

She nodded. "Sort of. I said he worked at this coffee shop."

She looked at me guiltily as I realized that it was a fifty-fifty chance—it could've been me lying dead on that floor.

"Wait, is that why he gave me that look when I saw you two at the Fish Camp?"

"Probably." She shrugged. "But what I'm trying to tell you is Scott didn't kill Ryan. At least, I don't think so."

"His car was seen leaving the island," I countered. "Why else would he be over there?"

"The girl he was seeing—is seeing. We lied to the police. We didn't decide to reconcile that night. We decided to split up. Or rather, I decided we should split up. I told him to just to get out of our house. He told me he went there, and they did their deeds. And when he told her he was there to stay, well, she wasn't ready for that kind of commitment."

Robin chuckled. "He was tossed out of two houses that night."

"Or so he claims," I said.

"But why didn't he tell the police that?"

"I think Scott thinks I did it. He thinks I caught Ryan with another woman. Then I killed them both. He's being chivalrous, if you'll believe it."

It was hard to believe.

"It doesn't make sense," I said. "Why would he take the blame for you when *you* kicked him out?"

"You'd have to know Scott. He takes responsibility for ruining our marriage."

"Ruining a marriage isn't worth a lifetime in prison," I said. "If Scott didn't do these things, then who did? You know it almost sounds like it could've been you."

I backed away, aware of where the Captain America bust was above my head, my only defense. I half expected her to raise a gun from her purse that very instant in some crazy attempt to kill anyone who suspected her of the crimes.

But she didn't.

"I really don't know who did it," she answered. "That's the God's honest truth. I was hoping you could help somehow. It sounds foolish now that I'm here. I think maybe I should go up to the police station. Maybe you're right. Maybe they'll arrest me. Charge me for both murders. But that's a chance I have to take. I'm sorry things turned out this way."

She gave Gambit one last awkward pat on his head, and she was out of the shop. My heart hammered in my chest for a while after that.

Every new customer startled me out of a daze. My head spun with questions. Was Robin being honest? Or was it all an act? Maybe she somehow knew Felicia and I were friends, and she was trying to send me, but really Felicia, off on a wild goose chase.

It had to be her or Scott, I thought. Either individually or together, they had something to do with this. I was convinced—or at least that's what I told myself for a little while.

22

"Are you okay?" Sarah waved her hand in front of my face.

"I'm all right. Why?"

"Because you look out of it. In fact, you've been out of it all day. You messed up two drinks, rung up the wrong order for Karen—Karen, *the* Karen. She hasn't had anything other triple cappuccino with light foam since the day I started. I could probably go on."

"Please don't," I begged.

"I thought you'd be happy. They caught the killer. That's good news, right?"

"I'm not really sure," I said, definitely unsure. I'd texted with Felicia throughout the day, or rather, I had sent her texts. She still hadn't responded to a one of them.

Today 10:15 AM
Robin Snider didn't happen to show up there, did she?

Today 10:32 AM
Cause she came by here...

Today 11:48 AM
Did you find anything out about the fingerprint?
What about my theory? Do you think they worked together?

Today 12:12 PM
Sorry if I'm bothering you...

Today 12:15 PM
But seriously, what's going on? Anything?

"I think you need to take the rest of the night off," Sarah said. "I can clean up around here before the big, uh, get together—what do you call it again? Just a game? Dungeons and Dragons, right? That's what they play on that show on Netflix."

"Stranger Things, yeah." I nodded. "It's just a game of D&D. Not a big deal."

I thought about calling it off in light of the turnaround in the case. But to everyone else involved, the turnaround would probably be deemed a good thing. It was just that Robin Snider's words were eating away at me.

"You've worked more than your fair share this week," I

told Sarah. "It's not right. I know. I've been meaning to post a job online. I really don't know what I'm going to do when you leave."

"About that," she said.

"About what?"

She leaned back up against the counter. "I don't think I'm going back to school."

"No," I shook my head emphatically, "you can't quit school to be an assistant manager at a coffee shop. That's beyond ridiculous."

She laughed. "That's not why I'm quitting school. I mean, yeah, I'll continue working here. But I realized that I don't need a degree to write plays. I can just write plays. In fact, not only plays. I've got ideas for novels, a TV sitcom, a bunch of things. I'd even like to try my hand at a comic book script. And with schoolwork, the ideas just stagnate. I never have time to work on them. But when I'm here..."

Sarah rested her hand on a spiral notebook behind her.

"You're sure you really want to stay here and do that?"

"Why not? It's the perfect place to write. I don't have to wait tables in LA to set my script under some producer's coffee. They have email. Anyway, I have to write it all down first. No use trying to skip a step."

"Right." I nodded. "Well, if that's how you feel, then the job's yours. Title and all."

"Assistant manager?" she asked for confirmation.

"Assistant manager," I confirmed, laughing. "But I'm not sure you can fit it on that name tag." It still read "ask me about Captain Marvel" above her name.

Above Sarah's head was the display shelf with figures and toys. It reminded me of something, and I reached out above her head. She ducked coolly away.

"What's that for?"

I set the Captain America statue on the counter beside the espresso machine.

"It's for Corey—if he shows up tonight with Marc. I think he deserves this. You know, after everything."

"You think Ryan would be okay with that?"

I shrugged. "Maybe not. But if Ryan wants me to continue selling comics then I have to do it my way."

"Fair enough." She smiled.

Today 5:16 PM
Still waiting...

Today 6:20 PM
Felicia Strong
Wow... I thought you were dating that girl from last night.
Haven't seen so many texts since I dumped Bud Miller in high school.
Really, I'm sorry. I left my personal cell in the car this morning. It's been quite the day. You have my other number, you know? Oh, so is it my turn to be ignored?

Today 6:26 PM
Felicia Strong
Kirby?

Today 6:30 PM

Felicia Strong

To answer your questions, yes Robin came in this morning (with her lawyer). She "corrected" her previous statements. And Scott withdrew his confession. That's all I can say for now. I'll stop by later - if I'm allowed? You got another big date lined up? ;)

Gambit needed a walk, so we headed to the park. He was a little less resistant this time. We got to the fenced in area, and I threw a tennis ball for him to chase. Being late afternoon on a hot summer day, we were the only two around.

I kept tapping the phone's home button, checking for missed messages. In fact, I'd been doing so all day. The battery had drained down to almost nothing. Then finally on the way back to the shop, it died completely.

"Figures," I said, stowing it in my back pocket. "She'll probably text back any minute."

Gambit tilted his head in reply.

"Yeah, yeah," I mumbled. "I don't even think it's weird anymore either."

"You don't think what's weird?" Sarah was just making her way out of the shop.

"Talking to him." I pointed to the dachshund.

"Of course it's not." Sarah's voice took on the high pitched tone of speaking to a child. She bent down to pet him. "Talking to animals is an age old tradition. It's when someone thinks they talk back... That's where there's a problem."

"Agreed," I said, grinning. I led Gambit on past the door and towards the Golf.

"Wait, you aren't going in?" she asked. But she pulled her keys to the store out.

"Nah, we're eating dinner with Memaw tonight. The usual Friday. I'll be back with plenty of time before the guys get here."

"Have fun." She grinned and locked up.

"Wait!" I stopped her. "You don't want to join us, do you?" I felt guilty for not thinking to ask her before.

"Oh, no. Definitely not. Comics I can do. I don't think I'm ready for role playing games."

"Suit yourself," I said. But I couldn't blame her. It'd been years since I'd played, and I was afraid I might have forgotten how to enjoy myself.

I just had to keep reminding myself it was a game and meant to be fun. What could possibly go wrong?

23

The lights were turned down. It was about quarter till nine. I expected the other guys to show up any minute. The shop had that late night coffee shop feel—like there could be an open mic night.

In fact, that was a pretty good idea. I put that on my ever-growing list of things to do.

Tonight, however, wasn't about poetry or songs. It was to honor Ryan—to honor him in a way he'd like to be honored.

Gambit curled up in his dog bed, still exhausted from our play at the park earlier. He was a sort of dungeon master in his own regard. Funny how I'd only truly gotten to know him after Ryan's death. Now he was as much a part of my life as Ryan had been—maybe even a better friend.

I had a couple lattes ready. One for me, one for Damian. My plan was win him over with a new drink—granted, almost any latte is better than plain black coffee. I knew Tim and Marc would probably opt for beer—you can't change some habits.

Tim rushed through the door excitedly, followed by Damian, who carried most of the supplies. It was only a little disappointing that neither dressed the part. Tim wore the same blue shirt while Damian was wearing something from Game of Thrones. Tyrion Lannister's quote: *That's what I do. I drink, and I know things.*

But Damian definitely wasn't of age. He was drinking a latte along with me. I handed it to him, and while his expression wasn't really a warm one, there were no longer eye daggers being propelled in my direction.

Marc arrived. I half expected or maybe hoped Corey would tag along. But Marc was alone. He held a six pack aloft for Tim's approval.

"The good stuff," Tim acknowledged.

We gathered around the booth, ready to play D&D. Miniatures and character sheets were laid out on the table. The twenty-sided die sat at the table's center.

The campaign was underway.

During it, Tim disallowed breaking character. He was worse than Ryan as a strict dungeon master. He was into it. He'd even written a ghost of Ryan's character into the plot. We all approved. It seemed Ryan would live on in multiple ways.

We took a break halfway through the campaign for the bathroom and more coffee. I thought it was a good time to check my phone and see if Felicia ever texted me back. I patted down my front pockets but nothing was there. Then I scoured the countertops and tables. Nothing.

"Crap," I whispered. I'd left it charging at Memaw's. Now I'd be anxious for the rest of the game. Hell, the rest of the night. I couldn't barge into Memaw's house at this hour.

"I'm sorry about the other day," Damian said. He didn't even seem to have been put up to it by his father. The words were genuine.

"No problem. I understand."

"I'm just glad they caught the guy. Why d'ya think he did it?"

"It's complicated," I answered, realizing it wasn't an answer at all. "Jealousy, maybe. He saw Ryan with his ex and he just snapped."

"People do go pretty crazy about girls," Damian agreed. "Don't know why he'd kill her then. To cover it up?"

I nodded. His guess was as good as mine. But Robin's words rang in the back of my mind.

"I know," Marc strode over, "it's unimaginable. Who would shoot Jill in cold blood like that?" Marc shook his head disapprovingly.

And oddly enough, my eyes caught on an issue of Ultimate Spider-Man in the display case as my spidey senses tingled. Felicia hadn't even told *me* how Jill died. *So how does Marc know?*

"Terrible, terrible world we live in," Tim said. "Let's talk about something else. Something good. How's the repairs on that boat coming along? When are you setting sail?"

"It's going," Marc said. He looked at me, understanding I wasn't tracking the conversation. "I bought Corey's sailboat the other day. He gave me a great deal. I showed it to them the other night at the wake."

"But you've been living in it for what, a month now?" Tim asked.

"Right," Marc looked at me again. "I just moved it from the slip at Corey's house. I felt like I was imposing. The plan is to sail around the Caribbean for a while. Get my mind right after all this mess."

Or to get away.

It was all starting to make sense. Too much sense.

"If I had the resources," Tim said, "I'd probably do the same."

"Sure you would," Damian interjected snidely.

"What? I would."

"Dad, you haven't been to the beach in five years. You really think you'd go sailing?"

"Well, I might." Tim huffed. "You guys get what I mean, right? I just don't have the resources you do, Marc."

"We get it." I nodded.

"All right, well, let's finish up here." Tim went back to his notes.

"Actually, Dad, I'm getting a little tired. You think we can continue next week?"

"I'm okay with it if Kirby is. I was thinking this might be a one time thing?"

All eyes went on me—including Marc's. A bead of sweat formed on my forehead. A feeling of unease washed over my entire being.

"Yeah, I'd love to play again," I answered. "I'm happy if we keep this tradition going."

"You are?" Marc asked, surprised.

"Of course," I said. "Anything to keep Ryan's memory alive."

This time I noticed it—the slight wince he made at the sound of Ryan's name. How had I missed that before?

"Sounds good." Tim began to clean things up. I did the same. Now wasn't the time to play hero. I couldn't let on that I knew anything. I would usher him out with the other two, and then go from there.

I'd seen enough episodes of *Castle* to understand never to put myself alone with the killer. Each episode needed a climax. But for me, a simple text to Felicia would suffice. *A text...* If only I actually had my phone to send one.

The shop's landline would do. I still had her card in my

wallet. I'd call her on her detective line—it was official police business after all.

I set the coffee cups down in the sink, emptied the beer bottles and put them in the trash. After Tim gathered up the figures and his notebook filled with both attached and loose paper, I walked with them to the door in a gaggle. I wanted all three to be out the door so I could lock up as swiftly as I was able.

Luckily, Marc wasn't dragging his feet. He wasn't trying to stay back—otherwise, I didn't know what I would do to dissuade the others from leaving.

"Y'all have a good night," I waved to them from the door.

I turned the lock and relief washed over me.

I made it behind the counter, pulled out my wallet and Felicia's card, and searched for cordless receiver of the landline.

Where did Sarah have it last?

Her apron was hanging on the hook behind the wall. I felt inside the pocket and found the phone. A low growl pierced the silence of the store and the bell on the door jingled softly.

I poked my head around the wall and found myself staring into the barrel of a 9mm pistol—the same pistol I had used to qualify as a marksman in the Air Force.

"Put the phone down, Kirby," Marc said in a hollow tone.

I put the phone down on the counter, right next to something else of value—something I'd forgotten about that afternoon.

Gambit had moved from growl to bark. He could feel the tension in the situation.

"Gambit," I called, grabbed the object, and raced for the back room. The dog scampered after me. But cold and calculating Marc made no such effort.

He gave me the time to scoop Gambit up and lock him in the office by himself. I slammed the door with emphasis.

"There's nowhere to hide back there," Marc said. "I'll make it quick."

"Who are you framing this time?" I asked while attempting not to give away my position. I managed to wedge myself at an angle he'd only see when entering the hallway. And even then, I hoped his eyes were on the office door.

"Oh, this one will be self-inflicted. That's why I'm not chasing after you like a madman."

But you are a madman!

I slowed my breathing. Marc's was a loud hiss through his nose as he crept behind the counter toward the office. I saw the gun before I saw him. It was trained on the closed office door.

"Be a man, Kirby. Come out and face me!"

I didn't reply. I tried not to make a sound. I still needed him to move forward by about two feet.

"You want to know where you were wrong?" He spoke loudly at the door. "You thought only Corey and Ryan had crushes on Jill in high school. She was the prom queen, for God's sake. Everyone loved Jill. And she loved me. Or she did for a while."

I knew I couldn't just stand there any longer. Sooner or later, he'd turn. Or worse, he'd shoot the gun into the office with Gambit. I took the chance, brought the statue of Captain America up high, and struck the back of Marc's head just as he had done to Ryan with that rock.

I don't know what I expected—I wasn't striking to kill. And it turned out I didn't use enough force to knock him out either.

But what I did was enough. It knocked him to the

ground, and the gun clattered to the floor, sliding toward the staircase to my apartment.

"You asshole," he said as I pounced on top of him. He struggled, reaching for the gun, but only a second passed before we heard them.

The sound of sirens just outside the building.

"You already called them?" he asked me, still crawling toward the gun.

"No, I did." We both turned to see Felicia standing behind the counter, her gun pointed down at both of us. "Kirby, why don't you come wait behind me."

She didn't have to tell me twice. I scooted toward her like a crab, managing to keep the line of sight between her and Marc clear. And to Marc's credit, he didn't make another move. Nor did he speak another word after Felicia read him his Miranda rights.

Moments later, the store was again flooded with uniformed police officers. But this time, the true culprit was taken in the back of Felicia's Impala.

24

"Oh my goodness. Kirby Jackson, you could've been killed," Memaw scolded. "My heart can't take another scare like that."

"What do you even mean?" I asked. "I'm telling you about it after the fact. It's not like you were there or I'm in mortal peril this minute."

"But just the thought of you with a gun pointed in your direction." She put her hand over her heart. "See, my heart's just-a-racing."

"Is that one word or three?" I joked.

I'd managed to come by and get the phone the day prior —worked my usual Saturday shift, all hours with only Jason, the part-timer, filling in during lunch. Memaw called later that evening, inviting me to Sunday lunch, saying she'd heard something that couldn't be true.

And she was right—because it wasn't true at all. The town gossip had painted a picture of me as some sort of hero tracking down the killer on my own, then facing off with him. Hardly a word of it was even close to the truth.

"I still can't believe your old buddy Marc. He's been to this house, hasn't he?"

I nodded. "A long time ago, yes."

"But why? He was always such a nice boy."

"That's where you're wrong," I said. "He instigated the fight between Corey and Ryan. I always kind of wondered why Ryan was okay still being his friend after that. Marc always played the side that would suit him best."

"Well, probably because Ryan was a nice boy."

"You're right about that. See, none of us knew Marc was dating Jill. Not even Corey. I guess he wanted to keep it a secret, and since none of us talked to Jill anymore, it didn't matter. Not until they broke up, and she started seeing Ryan."

"Jealousy," Memaw said, matter-of-factly.

"Right. He must've seen Ryan coming out of her house and just snapped. Then he thought he had the perfect plan."

"To frame you."

I nodded. "It almost worked. Well, maybe not almost. But it sure didn't feel good to be on that side of the law. He was probably sweating bullets when they let me go. Jill would eventually point the police his way—it was only a matter of time. So he had to kill her, too."

"What a shame." Memaw shook her head.

"It really is," I agreed. "Three lives, if you count Marc's, ended over something so petty."

"Almost four." She took my hand lovingly into both of hers on the dining room table. The empty dining room table.

"So, uh, what was this lunch you promised?"

"Oh, that?" She gave me a guilt-ridden smile. "I probably have some leftovers in the fridge."

I couldn't say the prospect of digging through used cottage cheese and margarine containers to find lunch was an appetizing one—Memaw had never seen the value in *real* Tupperware.

"Mo's Hideaway it is," I said. "My treat."

"I never can eat a whole slice there," she said grudgingly, but not so grudging as to prevent her from standing and gathering her purse.

I followed her out, thinking it did seem like a ham and pineapple sort of day.

A few hours later, I was back with Gambit at the shop, my belly still full with one and a half slices of pizza. We were doing some inventory of the comics section. Or at least that's what I told myself I was doing. I'd gotten sidetracked and perused at least three issues. It seemed comics had come a long way since I was a kid. The stories more complex. The characters actually had flaws. They didn't always save the day—just most of the time.

There was a *knock knock* on the shop door. Gambit ran over, tail wagging.

Felicia stood there with the Captain America bust in her hands.

"We're closed today," I said jokingly.

She stepped inside, saw what I was up to, and laughed.

"They're better than I remember."

"I'm sure they are," she said. Felicia held the bust out toward me. "This belongs to you. It's not needed as evidence."

I took it in one hand. It felt heavier than I remembered.

"I think I'm going to give it to Corey. He'll appreciate it more than I will."

"It saved your life," she interjected dramatically.

"Right. But I don't really want that reminder.

She gave me a slight nod of understanding. "You know, I think last night was the first night I've truly slept in weeks. What about you?"

"Same," I said. "You do look a lot more refreshed."

"Thanks. That's really what a girl wants to hear. Oh, you look a lot less ragged and tired today than you have the past two weeks." Her voice was mocking.

"That's not exactly what I said." I laughed.

"Same difference." She laughed with me. "Hey, I really didn't mean to ruin your date the other night..."

Felicia looked at me with a guilty smile. *She should be guilty*, I thought. But only briefly. I was sour, but it wasn't all her fault Avett left as she did. While I hadn't heard from her since, Avett had at least added me as a friend on Facebook the next day.

"Sorry," Felicia said. "I saw the lights on. I thought you might be working or something. I really didn't think—"

"You didn't think I'd bring a date here? This place is actually a bit cleaner than upstairs. Plus, I'm not sure I'm ready to invite anyone upstairs just yet. You may have gotten me out of an awkward situation."

"Really? Still?" Felicia acted as if I was an odd duck. "Wasn't your breakup over a year ago?"

"It was," I nodded. "God, this is why I hate small towns. At least I had the luxury of explaining the whole situation to Avett. Your knowledge is what? Second or thirdhand at best?"

Felicia made a face. "Actually, it's more like fourth or fifth. My mom told me, and who knows where she heard it."

"I can carve out some time to explain. I mean, if you're interested." I wanted Felicia to be interested. "In fact," I said. "I'd love to hear more about you—you know like almost anything other than your life as a detective. I think we've covered that one, tenfold."

"You mean you want to catch up like *real* friends?"

"Exactly." I nodded.

"I'd like that. Actually, Kirby, I'd like that a lot."

Please consider leaving a review.

Find out what's next for Kirby, Gambit, and crew in *Lattes and Lies*, Comics and Coffee Case Files Book 2.

For new releases, updates, and more, sign up to the newsletter.

ABOUT CHRISTINE ZANE THOMAS

Christine Zane Thomas is the pen name of a husband and wife team. A shared love of mystery and sleuths spurred the creation of their own mysterious writer alter-ego.

While not writing, they can be found in northwest Florida with their two children and schnauzer, Tinker Bell. When not at home, their love of food takes them all around the South. Sometimes they sprinkle in a trip to Disney World. Food and Wine is their favorite season.

ABOUT WILLIAM TYLER DAVIS

After leaving the Shire, William "Tyler" Davis was an exchange student at Hogwarts School of Witchcraft and Wizardry. Sorted into Ravenclaw house, he spent many years there before taking time off to companion the Doctor around space and time. He found his wife Jenn while searching wardrobes for Narnia. They settled down in Florida (of all places) to begin adventures with two halflings that like to call them Mommy and Daddy.

After ten years of half-finished stories, he finally finished something. He stored that one away.

Then he wrote the Epik Fantasy series, a humorous fantasy about a halfling who wants to be a wizard.

A lover of *The Hardy Boys* and *The Cat Who*, *Comics and Coffee Case Files* is his first cozy mystery series.

ACKNOWLEDGMENTS

There are so many people I'd like to thank for their help.

Jenn, my love, my alpha reader, always helps keeps track of the little things.

Ellen, my editor, thanks for keeping track of the *big* things.

My mom, my proofreader, finds the typos when everyone else's eyes glance of (or should that be off) them.

And finally, thanks to Jason, my first reader, for trying out a new genre.

Made in the USA
Lexington, KY
21 July 2019